THE EMERALD
EYES OF DEATH

*A Violet Vaughn Southwestern
Mystery #2*

Kristina Charles

Ulm Publishing

Cover design by: ULM Publishing
Library of Congress Control Number: 2018675309
Printed in the United States of America

CONTENTS

CHAPTER 1

Take it Easy blared from the radio of the bright blue Mini Cooper convertible. The four friends zoomed down a desolate desert highway, singing the Eagles hit at the top of their lungs. The cool, fragrant morning air zipped through Violet's hair, but she didn't mind the chill. In the side mirror, she saw her dog's head poking out the window, eyes closed, enjoying the desert smells and embodying his name—Spirit. Violet belted out the last line of the chorus and noticed Hugh at the wheel, looking over at her as if he was singing the words to her only.

Maven yelled something from the backseat, so Hugh turned the music down.

"You need to pull over around the next turn. Scenic marker."

Just as she spoke, the turnout came into view and Hugh guided the Mini onto a semi-circle of pavement. Violet, Hugh, Maven, Maddie and Spirit all piled out of the car. Violet closed the door and caught her reflection in the window. What a difference a few months made. She adjusted the tan-colored cowboy hat over her dark, blunt-cut bob. The clean air and ample time outdoors brought a rosy glow to her middle-aged skin. Binoculars hung around her neck and she clutched two guidebooks in her hand, one for local birds, the other plants. Maddie told her she could get all the information in an app, but it wasn't the same. She loved her books, now dog-eared and full of page markers. She wore cargo pants, which she had come to appreciate for the many pockets to store whatever treasures she found. She looked like, well—a local.

The group began to wander toward the guard rail. Violet approached and sucked in her breath. The vista overlooked a valley which seemed like something out of a Dr. Seuss book. Gray, white and tan hills pushed up between flatlands that sprouted an array of weird formations, twisted and curved as if dolloped out of a pastry bag. The nature-made monolithic pillars came in all sizes, from the height of a human to craggy, deformed giants. Red and pink lines swept across the sides of canyons and mountains as if swiped with a paintbrush. Violet smelled a salty, mineral scent in the air.

"Badlands." Maven beamed, pride in the local landmark radiating on her face.

When Violet came to Coatimundi, New Mexico a few months ago, she hit it off with Maven and her partner Maddie right away, bonding over their love of the desert. The two had also been a huge support when Violet and Hugh ran into trouble in the tiny town. Now that she thought about it, she had only known Hugh for the same amount of time, and yet, it seemed like so much longer than that. They were close friends now. Was friends the right word? That was a subject she was struggling with.

Violet and Hugh oohed and ahhed at the spectacular view before them.

Maddie pointed off to the right. "Look out over there, Violet. See, that's Three Peaks. Your trailer is right on the other side."

Maven pointed in the other direction. "And right down there is where we're headed. Emerald Eyes Hot Springs."

"I do wish you would finally tell us why they call it Emerald Eyes," said Hugh in his proper British accent. "The suspense is killing me." He peered over the side in the direction Maven pointed.

"You'll know when you see it," said Maven. "Now let's go, I can't wait. It's not often I get to show our hidden gem to someone for the first time." Maven's last few words were almost drowned out by the sound of a big rig gravel truck rumbling by, followed by a water tanker truck. Violet called Spirit to her and held his collar, worried he might run into the road.

"That's strange," said Maven. "You don't often see any traffic out here, let alone trucks."

Back in the car, they wound down the twisty road. When they reached the valley, Maven pointed where Hugh should turn onto an almost-hidden dirt trail. A small wooden sign, held to a post with wire, read simply "hot springs" with an arrow. The big trucks must have come this way because a cloud of dust hung in the air. They had gone barely fifty yards before Maven yelled, "Stop!"

Hugh slowed the Mini to a standstill. The dust clouds cleared to reveal a massive, newly-erected billboard. The sign depicted a colorful rendering of a modern community with palm trees, swimming pools and a golf course. Black lettering at the top read: Future Home of Emerald Eyes Luxury Community!

Maven's door flew open. She sprung out of the car and stomped toward the sign. She stood underneath the monstrosity and looked up. "What is this?" she yelled. "What. Is. This? No, no, no, no, no, no, no!"

The water truck had splashed a trail of liquid on its route. Maven bent down and grabbed a glob of muddy sand and threw it at the sign. It landed on one of the swimming pools, leaving a murky brown splat. Maddie exited the car and walked up to her partner, placing a hand on her shoulder in what couples around the globe recognize as *calm down, before you get in trouble*. She guided Maven back to the car and they both got in.

Hugh continued up the road then looked in the rearview mirror. "I'm sorry, Maven. Sometimes we just can't stop progress—even out here."

Maven sat in the back seat, arms crossed. "Wanna bet?"

Construction vehicles appeared to be flattening a large area near the billboard. As the Mini moved on, the sounds of progress began to fade away.

After a few miles of bumpy road and silence Maven spoke up from the back of the car. "I'm sorry to ruin everyone's day. I know, I'm acting like a baby. I was so excited to show you this place and now—it's ruined."

Violet reached into the back of the car, grabbed her friend's hand and squeezed it. "You haven't ruined anything."

The road passed between a crevice barely wide enough for the car. Hugh pulled to a stop. Violet gasped at the flat open area made of salty-looking smooth white stone. Towering cliffs, laced with holes and alcoves, encircled the open space like the Colosseum. In the middle, like a pair of gleaming cat eyes, twin emerald green pools of water glimmered in the sun. Steam rose from the hot springs creating a mystical vision.

"Oh. My. Gosh," breathed Violet. "It looks like something from a sci-fi movie."

"Why is the water so green?" asked Hugh.

"It's some kind of combination of the minerals," said Maddie. "It's completely safe to soak in. But stay away from the smaller clear pool near the side of the cliffs. That's called The Djinn."

"I wouldn't mind falling into a pool of gin," said Hugh, "Sounds like quite a party."

Maddie laughed. "It sounds like gin, but it's spelled with a D. It's a mythological demon. That water is boiling hot and you can't get out if you fall in. Keep Spirit away from it too. It has a chain around it and a sign, but every few years some fool falls in."

"Don't fall into the gin!" Hugh called out the window, to which Violet and Maddie laughed with hilarity. Maven wasn't in the joking mood—she stared stone-faced out the window.

Hugh pulled the car off the road into a clearing. When Violet opened her door, the pungent odor of sulfur hit her.

"You get used to it," said Maddie, noticing Violet's wrinkled nose.

The group got their cooler and tote bags from the trunk and hiked the short distance to the pools. Maven lagged behind and Maddie called back to her. "Come on Mave, shake it off. Let's enjoy our time here."

Maven picked up her pace and caught up with the group. "You're right, I'm gonna enjoy it. While I can." She started to remove her T-shirt then looked at Hugh and Violet devilishly. "No swimsuits allowed out here. We go in the pools as nature intended."

CHAPTER 2

Violet felt panic wash over her and Hugh's jaw dropped.

Maven then pulled off her shirt to reveal a tie-dye one piece swimsuit. "Gotcha!" She ran barefoot over the smooth stone surface to the edge of the pool.

Violet breathed a sigh of relief. She felt her own swimsuit digging into her skin underneath her clothes. She ordered it online, specifically for this excursion. It was supposed to be guaranteed to take off ten pounds. She felt like a sausage ready to burst out of its casing, but right now she wished she had a suit that would take off twenty pounds. During the weeks of getting her restaurant ready, she sampled a few too many recipes. Now she felt self-conscious, especially in front of Hugh.

He didn't appear to have the same reservations. He had already stripped off his shirt and pants and sat next to Maven, dipping his feet in the water. "Come on!" he called. He had a farmer's tan from doing a lot of work outside over the past weeks. He did not have the muscled form of an Adonis, but she found his dad bod to be pleasingly solid.

She stripped down to her swimsuit and quickly

wrapped a towel around her waist. It was definitely diet time. She walked to the edge of the hot spring and sat down next to Hugh. Maven and Maddie were already in the water, eyes closed, enjoying the heat.

"I was waiting for you," said Hugh, taking her hand. "Let's go in together."

She took off her towel and the two of them slid into the water. It enveloped her skin, just the perfect temperature, right on the edge of hot and too hot. She closed her eyes and felt all tension and self-consciousness melt away. "Ahh," she said, breathing out a long, slow breath.

After a good soak, the friends spread out a blanket and lounged in the sun, eating the snacks Violet prepared. She used the opportunity to test out a few recipes for her restaurant which was set to open next week.

First, an antipasto salad with juicy tomatoes, cucumbers, salami, chunks of mozzarella and lemon vinaigrette. Next, chicken salad sandwiches on focaccia bread. The bread was a new creation, pillowy and cheesy, made with local hatch chiles. Finally, Violet brought out a plastic cake caddy and unveiled what she hoped would be one of the restaurant's features: Southwestern chocolate cake. She found an interesting type of Mexican cocoa at a farmer's market in Albuquerque. The vendor told her the recipe was passed down for generations in his family. The cocoa had hints of cinnamon and nuts. It baked into a rich, dark chocolate cake.

She scanned the faces of her test subjects and

was gratified to see and hear signs of appreciation, as they mmm'd with eyes closed. She served a chunk to herself. The diet starts tomorrow, right?

Her eyes wandered to the surrounding cliffs and their odd, cut-out features. Way at the top of a high peak, she noticed a white, rounded structure built into the rocks.

"What's that building up there?"

Everyone looked to where she pointed.

"That's a stellar observatory," said Maddie. The scientists come into town sometimes. I think they're from one of the universities."

Hugh's face lit up. "I'd love to go up there. Is it open to the public?"

"No, it's private. I've heard rumors they do some top secret stuff. Of course, everyone around here says it has to do with aliens." She gave a snorting laugh.

Maven scowled. "You never know."

Maddie rolled her eyes. This appeared to be an area the two didn't agree on.

On the way back to the car, Maddie showed Hugh and Violet the hot spring known as The Djinn. Violet clipped a leash on Spirit and kept him close as they stepped carefully to the edge of a chain rail. A sign read: Danger. Scalding Water.

"I see what you mean," said Hugh, looking down into the clear pool. "The sides are practically vertical. If someone fell in, it would be impossible to get out."

It gave Violet the creeps, so she and Spirit went back to where Maven waited near the car. Maven was inspecting something in the rocks and waved her over.

"Look at this!"

Violet came closer and saw Maven pointing at a cute, fuzzy little cactus sticking out of the rocks. The squat, spiny plant sprouted one pinkish buff-colored bloom.

"Mesa Verde Cactus," Maven whispered in awe. "They're almost extinct. I haven't seen one of these in ages."

Violet excitedly pulled out her plant book and flipped through the pages. "Yes, it's right here. It says it's endangered."

Maven stared at the cactus, rubbing her chin in thought.

Hours later, the group zipped back down the highway toward Coatimundi, all of them markedly relaxed, melting into their seats. All of them except Maven, who sat up straight, fingers punching at her cell phone.

Maddie called out to Hugh. "I love your little car, Hugh, it's sweet!"

"With all the driving around I'm doing for my book, I needed a better car. No offense to your old pickup truck—and Violet needs the truck to get back and forth from the mesa."

In fact, Violet bought the truck from Maven for $100, which, Maven said, was $99 more than it was worth. Hugh was writing a book about a series of murders that occurred in the neighboring town of White Feather in the Navajo Nation. Their friend Dr.

Kai Wauneka's sister was one of the victims.

"What are you doing?" Maddie said, as she watched Maven's fingers flying over the phone keyboard.

"I'm texting Tamara. We're calling an emergency meeting of the Desert Preservation Society. Whoever's trying to ruin Emerald Eyes—they're not gonna get away with it."

Dr. Tamara Goodwill ran the Coatimundi hospital. She appeared every bit the straight-laced doctor by day. Violet came to find out the woman had a free-spirited, bohemian side. She saw the doctor several times on her days off dressed in long hippie skirts like Maven's, her naturally-styled afro accessorized with vibrant scarves, a crochet bag slung across her hip. Dr. Goodwill was also running for mayor, opposed by none other than Red Clayton, the wealthy rancher.

Violet sucked in her breath in shock as a thought occurred to her. "My hat! I've forgotten my hat back at the hot springs!"

It wasn't just any hat. It had been a special gift from Kai and Grace Wauneka, when she and Hugh narrowly survived an attack from a murderer. After arriving in the small town of Coatimundi in search of Violet's estranged husband, they became the top suspects in a double murder. Violet's quick thinking had led to the true culprit. The Wauneka's, a brother and sister from the neighboring Navajo Nation, presented Violet with the hat, adorned with Great Horned Owl feathers, symbolizing wisdom.

"I'll take you back there right now," said Hugh, slowing the car.

"I can't. I have to meet the people dropping off my new walk-in fridge at the restaurant. They're driving in all the way from Albuquerque."

Maddie patted her shoulder. "It'll be okay. Very few people go out there."

"Tell you what," said Hugh. "First thing tomorrow morning, we'll head out there and get it. I'll pack a picnic for us."

The thought of losing the hat gnawed away at her insides. She would be devastated to lose it. How could she have been so careless?

CHAPTER 3

Some people in Coatimundi thought Violet was crazy to move into the same trailer where she found her estranged husband dead. Violet sometimes felt a little crazy too. But in the end, practicality won out. Jim had a beautiful, brand new airstream trailer on his property, fancier than Violet's apartment in Chicago. Her second-hand RV wasn't even in the same class. Plus, Spirit needed space. Kai Wauneka, the veterinarian, said a border collie needed property and a job to do. He wouldn't be happy cooped up in the RV for long.

When Jim died, Violet became the owner of his property out on the mesa. She was also due a settlement from the sale of her house in Chicago—the one Jim had swindled away from her. Special Agent Montoya from the FBI informed Violet it would take time to realize the money—the case needed to make its way through the court system. Until that time, she needed to work with what she had.

In order to move to Coatimundi permanently and open her restaurant, she ended up selling a piece of her property to Red Clayton. He wanted the whole thing. In the end, both walked away satisfied with the deal. He got some of his Clayton property back and she had a piece of land of her very own.

Her new Coatimundi family stepped up to help her once again. Hugh, Maven, Maddie, Kai, Grace and a host of others came out one weekend and overhauled the trailer, getting rid of Jim's stuff, cleaning it and bringing in hand-me-down household items.

Maven pulled her aside and said, "This place needs to be saged, and pronto." Seeing Violet's blank look she continued. "You burn sage inside the house to rid it of all the bad energy. It's also called smoke cleansing or smudging. Anyway, this place needs it. I'll head home and get what we need. We'll do the ceremony tonight. You can't sleep here until it's done."

Maven performed the ritual, lighting a bundle of sage and walking through the trailer, wafting it here and there. Violet wasn't sure if it was the cleaning, the redecorating or the sageing, but afterwards she didn't feel afraid to be in the airstream or on the property. Quite the opposite. She felt like she was home.

The morning after they visited Emerald Eyes, Violet woke up early. The first thing she always did was listen for the windmill. She had come to think of the rusty old thing as a friend, a protector watching over her. When she received her settlement, besides building a new home on her property, she planned to refurbish the windmill.

Two blue eyes peered over the edge of the bed.

"I know, I'm coming," she said. The lack of a screeching sound from the windmill meant a quiet and still morning. She padded the short distance from the bedroom to the kitchen and opened the front door. Spirit flew outside for his morning romp. Violet joined him a short time later, coffee cup in hand, wrapped in a hooded sweatshirt. She sat in a folding chair in her new patio area and spent a pleasant morning looking through her bird book, trying to identify a falcon she had seen perched on a fence post.

The sound of her cell phone jarred her out of her reverie. The young, cherubic face of Gabriel, her new restaurant manager, gazed out from her phone screen. Facetime? Why did these young people always want to Facetime? She didn't like the way the phone camera distorted her face–and it was the phone camera, she was sure of it–especially this early in the morning. She answered it as an audio-only call."

"Sorry, Mrs. Vaughn, I forgot you don't like to Facetime."

Violet smiled at his sweet, earnest voice. "It's okay, what's going on?"

"My Uncle Kyle says he's got a batch of Big Jim peppers that just came in. They're so good, we should get some while we can."

Gabriel was the nephew of Violet's friend from the Navajo Nation, Kyle Dodge, also known as Dr. Pepper. When she decided to open a restaurant, she knew she'd need a good manager, since she had zero experience. Gabriel had been working at a fast food place in White Feather since he was sixteen and had been a manager since eighteen. He was eager to get out of fast food and came highly recommended from his uncle. She knew she'd made the right choice–he cared about Deep Dish just about as much as she did.

"Yes, let's do it," she said. "I'm glad you called. I've got to go back out to the hot springs this morning, I left my hat out there. Can you hold down the fort?"

"Sure, no problem. Any leads on a cook?"

"Not yet. I can do a lot of it, but I'm worried about the opening night–I think we might get a crowd."

"I put it out on social media. Don't worry, it'll all come together."

After the phone call, Violet looked around for Spirit. She spotted him standing frozen in the driveway, head cocked, looking out over the sage brush in the direction of the Clayton ranch. What was he was onto? She began to feel a slight vibration in the ground that turned into a rumble. Spirit started to bark. Violet walked out to where he stood but couldn't see anything. But in the distance, she could hear a beeping sound like some kind of heavy equipment backing up.

"We'll have to check that out later," she said to her dog. "Hugh will be here soon, I have to get dressed."

Hugh picked her up in the Mini and the two headed out to Emerald Eyes to retrieve the hat.

Violet reached over and patted Hugh's shoulder. "I feel like we've hardly seen each other." She said it lightly, but inwardly, she didn't feel very light about it. She almost wondered if Hugh had been avoiding her.

"Between your restaurant and my book, I think

we have our hands full," he said pragmatically. "And you moved out to the mesa while I'm still at Maven's Haven."

Was that it, she wondered. Was he feeling abandoned? Or was she just reading too much into things? She felt more than friendly toward Hugh, but sometimes she just couldn't tell with him.

"I do have some news," he said. "My daughter's coming to visit me in a few days. I'm sure the two of you will hit it off."

Oh, okay, Violet thought. Maybe he needs his daughter's approval before he goes any further. She chose to take it as a good sign that he wanted to introduce her to the most important person in his life.

They turned onto the dirt road leading to the hot springs and were pulled up short by the vision before them. Cars lined one side of the narrow road, leaving barely enough room for them to get through. Up ahead, near the billboard, they saw a group of people. As they came closer, Violet realized most of the group held up signs. The first one she saw read "Save the Cactus!"Another said "Hands off Our Desert!"

"Look!" said Violet. "A news truck! And—there's Maven!"

"Let's see what's going on," said Hugh, pulling his car to the side like the others.

They walked toward the group of about twenty people. Some of them were chanting, led by Maven. "One, two, three! Down with D.P.D.! One, two three! Down with D.P.D!"

Maven waved at them and hurried over. "Isn't

it great?" she beamed. "We got all this together in one night. Wait 'til the word gets out, we'll have even more." Maven wore a bright green knit cap on her head in the shape of a cactus.

"What's D.P.D.?" asked Hugh.

"Dewer Property Development. They're the ones doing the construction out here. Look, all the work's come to a standstill. Whenever a truck pulls up, we form a human chain and they can't get through."

Violet looked over to where they had seen construction work going on the previous day. The workers in their bright green shirts sat next to their equipment or stood talking in groups. She had a bad feeling in the pit of her stomach. Whoever was paying the men would not be happy.

"Tamara's getting interviewed for the news," Maven cried with glee. "It's Cody Blackstone from News 4 Albuquerque!" She hurried off again to lead the chant.

They moved closer to where Tamara stood next to a news reporter who held a microphone toward her.

"Certain people think they can sneak past local regulations to destroy our desert," Tamara said. "The Mesa Verde cactus is almost extinct. A development here would most certainly wipe it out. We've contacted the United States Fish and Wildlife Service and asked for a hold to be placed on this project. As mayor of Coatimundi, I would stop any project that threatened our desert way of life."

"Red Clayton's gonna have a hard time beating

that campaign speech," Hugh whispered. As if called by magic, a shiny white Range Rover barreled up the road and came to a halt in front of the group.

Red Clayton himself got out of the passenger side, his auburn hair glinting in the bright morning light. The driver, a tan man in his sixties with white hair and a yellow polo shirt emerged, his face flushed as red as Clayton's hair.

"Things are about to get ugly," said Hugh.

Cody Blackstone must have realized the same because he stopped his interview with Tamara and whispered to his cameraman who swung the camera around to the men.

The white-haired man yelled to the group in general. "What's going on? Why have my men stopped working?" A vein pulsed in his temple. Violet saw the logo on his shirt—D.P.D. This must be Mr. Dewer.

Maven marched up to the men, her loose skirt swaying, the limbs of her cactus hat bouncing up and down.

"Clayton," she spat. "I should have known you'd have your fingers in this pot."

"Maven," he said with a smile. "Don't you have some crystals to read or something?"

Tamara came to stand next to Maven. "Hello Clayton. You here to show the Coatimundi community how you skirt the rules and destroy landmarks?"

"Dr. Goodwill, as I'm sure you're aware, I own this property. Well, co-own with Mr. Dewer here." He noticed the camera and broadened his smile.

"Coatimundi is a dying town. We need to bring in new blood to revitalize this place. People don't want to come out here and live in trailers. They want swimming pools, golf courses. The businesses of Coatimundi are gonna thank me. *You're* gonna thank me, Maven."

"I'd rather kiss a lizard than thank you, Red Clayton."

Mr. Dewer stepped forward, waving his arms at the gathering. "Get outta here, you hippies! You're costing me thousands!"

"It's gonna cost you more than that," said Maven. "I guarantee it."

CHAPTER 4

"That Maven is a real firecracker," said Hugh as he parked the Mini in the same dirt area as the previous day. This time, they weren't alone at the hot springs. Another vehicle, a red jeep, was parked in the same area, but the occupants were nowhere to be seen.

"That's what I love about her," said Violet. "She's not afraid to tell the world how she feels. And she's right—A big development would ruin this place."

Spirit explored the desert joyfully, while Hugh and Violet grabbed the tote bags from the trunk— the picnic Hugh promised. A cloud passed over the sun, dimming the late morning light. Violet looked up toward the observatory on the cliff and saw slate gray sky.

"It looks like a storm's rolling in. We'd better find my hat before our picnic gets rained out."hh

"Agreed," said Hugh, "We don't want to get stuck on this dirt road in a downpour."

They headed toward the emerald green hot spring pools. As they came closer, two figures could be seen on the far side of the first pool. The two hot springs were separated by a rock formation, almost like a nose, rising up between the two eyes. It appeared to be a young couple, holding hands, as they maneuvered the uneven ground. The young man wore the same bright green shirt as the workmen on the D.P.D. project. The young woman wore jeans, a T-shirt and a cowboy hat.

"My hat!" Violet cried, "That girl has my hat!"

Hugh squinted. "You can tell from all the way back here?

"Yes, I'd know it anywhere. Follow that hat!"

Violet cupped her hands to her mouth and yelled, "Hey!" The couple didn't seem to hear her.

Violet and Hugh quickened their pace, closing some distance as the young people picked their way over the rocks. They rounded the first pool just in time to see their targets disappear.

They climbed up, following a path cut into the crumbly earth. Near the top of the short incline, the trail veered around a large boulder. In the lead, Violet proceeded around the boulder and then stopped in her tracks.

The teenagers sat on the edge of an outcropping, holding hands, their backs to Violet and Hugh. Violet knew the girl's flaming red hair anywhere, even underneath her hat. She held up a hand to stop Hugh and grabbed Spirit's collar, leading him back the way they had come.

"Bailey Clayton," she mouthed to Hugh.

"Who?" Hugh mouthed back.

"Red Clayton's daughter, Bailey," she whispered. "And a young man."

They sat for a moment with their back against the rock, Violet holding Spirit.

"Let's just go get the hat," said Hugh. He was starting to get an impatient look on his face that said he could care less about what the kids were doing and wanted to move on with the agenda. But Violet had an urge to see what Red Clayton's daughter was up to.

They heard the young man speak, a little muffled, but they could make it out. "So have you told your father yet?" There was a long pause. "That's what I thought. Are you chicken, or is it something else?" There was a teasing ring to his voice.

"It's just—my dad is kind of—complicated. He doesn't think anyone is good enough for me."

"But especially me."

"Don't say that. I will tell him. I will. What about you, have you told your mom?"

"Um—well, not exactly. Hey, let's not waste our time talking about this, I gotta get back to the worksite soon. The foreman gave us a break until they clear out those protestors, but I should be getting back."

"So, you haven't told your mom then," she said. "Oh, don't pout, come on, give me a kiss before you go."

Hugh's eyes looked like they would roll right out of his head. He gestured to Violet to get the hat. "Let's go," he mouthed, then pointed at the sky. "Rain."

She nodded in agreement. She had indulged her curiosity long enough. But now Spirit looked down at the base of the rocks. A low growl rumbled in his throat. They heard some other distant voices near the first pool. Two men came into sight, involved in a heated discussion. Red Clayton and Mr. Dewer.

"It's gonna happen, Clayton—whether you're on board or not." Dewer pointed to the edge of the hot spring. "You see all this uneven ground? That's got lawsuit written all over it. You stick to sheep farming and let me handle the development."

"We're in this fifty-fifty, Dewer. And I'm running for mayor. The town's never gonna—"

"Fifty one-forty nine, if I'm not mistaken. Advantage—me."

The men stopped as they noticed Violet and Hugh, backs to the boulder, holding Spirit's collar. Red's eyes widened. Then he tipped his hat. "Mrs. Vaughn. Dr. Gordon."

Crunching sand and laughter came from behind the boulder and seconds later, Bailey and her boyfriend emerged, holding hands, ready to descend the incline. Silence fell. Violet watched a range of emotion pass over Red's face, from confusion to surprise to anger.

Bailey dropped the young man's hand. "Dad! What are you doing here?"

"What am *I* doing here? I'm working. What are *you* doing here? With—that Matt character?"

Violet and Hugh's heads moved back and forth as they became the meat in an awkward sandwich.

"His name's Mateo, Dad. Mateo. His mom's only worked for you for like, twenty years."

"Get down here," Red grumbled. "Now. You too, Matt or Mateo or whatever your name is."

The teens scrambled down the incline, as only

kids can, passing Hugh and Violet without even seeing them.

Then Dewer spoke up. "You—" He pointed at Mateo. "You work for me? Why aren't you out at the site?"

Mateo straightened his broad shoulders and looked Dewer in the eye. He really is a handsome young man, Violet thought. No wonder Bailey had her heart stolen.

"The foreman gave us a break because those people blocked our work. My girlfriend brought me some lunch."

"Girlfriend?" said Red, looking the most disconcerted Violet had ever seen him.

"Yes, said Mateo, taking Bailey's hand. "Girlfriend."

"Listen, son," said Dewer. "I guess you don't know the golden rule of construction—or any business for that matter. You don't mess with the owner's daughter. You're fired, kid."

"*What?*" Mateo and Bailey spoke at the same time. Then Bailey turned on her father.

"No, Dad, it's not fair, he didn't do anything!"

Mateo addressed Dewer. "Please, sir. I do a good job for you. I haven't missed a day of work. I really need this job."

"We all have our little problems today, kid. Get lost."

Mateo let go of Bailey's hand and strode off, clipping Dewer's shoulder as he passed. "It's not fair!" he yelled. It echoed off the canyon walls, scattering some crows who joined in with loud, screeching caws.

"Mateo!" Bailey called, moving to follow him.

Red grabbed her arm. "Don't even think about it."

Hugh took Violet's hand and they descended the incline. Violet let go of Spirit and he bounded down to the group below.

"Terribly sorry," said Hugh. "Don't mean to interrupt. We're just here to retrieve Violet's hat. Miss—if you please," he pointed at the hat on Bailey's head.

Bailey, obviously surprised at their appearance, removed the hat and handed it over.

"Well then—carry on," said Hugh.

They hurried past, heading back toward the car, just as the first splashes of rain hit. Violet pulled her special hat onto her head and immediately felt better.

Hugh winked at her. "Mission accomplished. But I think the picnic's off."

"It's okay, we can go eat at my place. There's too many weird vibes out here today."

Hugh laughed. "Just another day in Crazymundi."

They ate their picnic out on Violet's covered patio, enjoying the delicious smell of fresh rain in the desert. Hugh brought fruit, chips and egg salad sandwiches, cut up in little triangles.

He held up one of the sandwiches. "These are my mum's specialty."

"Delicious. Maybe I can put a Southwestern

twist on them and serve them in the restaurant."

"You seem to be expanding from deep dish pizza."

"I know, it's—evolving. But pizza will still be the main focus. Speaking of that, tomorrow's the Desert Harvest Day thing in town. You wanna help me pass out flyers for my new restaurant?"

"Desert harvest seems like an oxymoron to me."

"I know, you don't think of the desert being flush with produce. But there's actually a lot of agriculture around here. There's squash, peppers, tomatoes—"

Hugh held up a hand. "I'm only teasing. Anyway, I have to fetch Bella from the airport, but we'll try to stop by when we get back. I'm at your service today, though. What do you say we have a go at hanging your lights."

Violet wanted twinkle lights exactly like the ones on Hugh's RV awning. They spent the afternoon outdoors, the project taking much longer than anticipated, as is often the case with anything involving strings of lights.

The sound of a car out on the dirt road caused Violet to pause in her work and shade her eyes from the afternoon sun. With such little traffic out here, the sound of any vehicle made her feel like a pioneer out on the prairie who spots a lone rider in the distance. If she spent much more time out here, she was sure she'd exclaim, "Well I'll be–who do you reckon that is?" like most of the other mesa dwellers.

Soon, her manager Gabriel's little silver Toyota

pulled up the drive and the young man got out, carrying a cardboard box. Spirit barked a greeting and bounded along beside him.

"The fliers came in," he called, as he bounced up the dirt drive. Gabriel was slight of build and short of stature, but big on presence. His straight black hair fell to his shoulders and he wore a flannel shirt, jeans and Converse.

They sat down in the folding chairs and Violet opened the box and pulled out a flier.

"They look so good! The logo's amazing." She handed one to Hugh.

"Very professional," Hugh agreed. "Say, what's this about a costume party?"

"Oh, I forgot to tell you. There's been so much going on. Since we're having our opening night on Halloween, we decided to make it a costume party."

"Oh." He sounded a little deflated. "That's–that's a brilliant idea. I'm sure the locals will love it."

Violet could sense Hugh was miffed that she hadn't shared her plans with him. But things were happening so fast, the past few months seemed like a blur.

Gabriel left and Violet checked the time on her phone. "Hey, let's try to catch the news. Maybe we can see Maven and Tamara."

"You wouldn't happen to have any more of that chocolate cake would you?" asked Hugh, seemingly over his momentary sulk.

"You're reading my mind."

Remembering the swimsuit situation, Violet

cut herself a tiny slice of cake and handed Hugh a large one. They settled into her cozy living room and she flipped on the TV.

A live shot filled the screen. Bright graphics surrounded Cody Blackstone, the reporter they saw earlier in the day. A red banner at the bottom read: Breaking News - Death at Emerald Eyes Hot Springs.

Violet's hand went to her chest. "Oh my gosh! I wonder what's happened!"

Her phone dinged with a text from Maddie. "Need help ASAP. Meet me at Badlands."

CHAPTER 5

Violet and Hugh hurried through the door of Badlands Barbecue, the gathering spot for most Coatimundi locals. A large group of regulars stared up at the TV. Maddie's pink hair stood out in the crowd and Violet rushed over.

"What's going on? Is Maven okay?"

Tears began to roll down Maddie's cheeks. Violet saw the Breaking News banner up on the TV and sucked in her breath. "Oh no! She's not—?"

Maddie followed her gaze. "No, no, she's alive, she's okay."

"Thank goodness," Hugh said. "You had us frightened."

"But it's not good either. She's at the sheriff's office. They think she had something to do with—that." She pointed up at the screen.

"What's it all about?" asked Violet. "Who died?"

Maddie lowered her voice. "A lot of people don't know this yet. The sheriff's trying to keep things quiet. They found that Dewer guy dead. Floating in the Djinn. Boiled alive."

Violet's hand flew to her mouth.

"How ghastly," said Hugh, putting an arm

around Violet.

"Was it—an accident?" asked Violet. "Did he fall in, like you warned us about?"

"It doesn't look like it. Maven says there were signs of some kind of scuffle and the man's sunglasses were crushed on the ground. I think—I think someone pushed him in."

Violet felt sick at the thought of anyone suffering that gruesome fate. "Who would do such a thing?"

Her eyes, and everyone's, turned to Cody Blackstone on the screen.

"Earlier today, this was quite a different scene, as protestors came out in force to block the construction of a controversial housing development." The screen cut away to a shot of Dewer, waving his arms at the group.

"Get outta here, you hippies! You're costing me thousands!"

The camera zoomed in on Maven's face as she responded to Dewer. "It's gonna cost you more than that. I guarantee it."

"That doesn't look good," said Hugh.

"Exactly," said Maddie. "Maven told half the county how angry she was. She's the one who organized the protest."

Hugh released a long breath. "All this talk about the Djinn—I need a martini."

"Get one for me as well," said Violet as she put an arm around Maddie.

Maddie put up a finger to indicate she was in.

"You better be gettin' one of those for me too," a familiar voice chimed in.

"Maven!" Maddie cried, and ran to give her a hug.

A cheer went up among the bar patrons and someone shouted, "We know you didn't kill that man, Maven!"

"So much for no one knowing about it," Violet whispered to Hugh.

Hugh ordered four martinis and joined Violet, Maddie and Maven at a pub table.

"So?" Maddie asked.

"The sheriff thinks I did it," said Maven. "I'm insulted. Just about everyone knows I'm a peace lover. Hell, I have a peace sign tattooed on my—"

"We don't need to tell them that," said Maddie. "The point is, you say you didn't do it, and I believe you."

"The sheriff kept saying they found evidence, but he wouldn't tell me what kind. But it can't be too much, because he let me go. For now, anyway."

Violet turned to Maddie. "You texted me earlier saying you needed help. What can I do?"

"You and Hugh were the first people I thought of. You got yourselves off the hook when you were in hot water."

Violet shuddered. "That might not be the best phrasing, considering."

"Oh, right. Sorry. I know how Sheriff Winters operates. Once he gets an idea in his head, he has tunnel vision."

"You're not wrong there," said Hugh.

Violet knew very well how Sheriff Winters did business, which made her wary of getting involved. She would prefer to stay off his radar. But Maddie and Maven had helped her when she was in trouble.

"There were a bunch of protestors there today at the entrance and several folks were out at the hot springs—including Hugh and me. I'm surprised the sheriff doesn't think we did it."

The door to Badlands swung open and voices hushed at the site of two law enforcement officers striding into the bar. Sheriff Winters wore his usual scowl, while the affable Deputy Jones smiled and nodded at the townsfolk. The sheriff's eyes scanned the room and landed on Violet. He made a beeline for their table.

Hugh whispered in Violet's ear. "You summoned the dragon."

Violet's shoulders drooped and all she could think was ugh. However long it had been since she faced off with Sheriff Winters, it hadn't been long enough. She still had nightmares about her short stay in the Coatimundi jail.

A tall redhead entered the bar. The eyes of the townsfolk, glued on the sheriff, were ripped away from that scene onto an even juicier one as the curvaceous woman called over to Sheriff Winters.

"Dan! There you are. I've been traipsing halfway to White Feather and back trying to track you down. You said you'd be home by dinnertime. And I made Frito pie."

A round of guffaws and sniggering erupted and a flush crept slowly up the sheriff's face. Jennifer, the red head, had been the mistress of Violet's deceased husband. But the whole town knew Sheriff Winters had been pining after her for years. The sheriff achieved his heart's desire around the time Violet first arrived in town.

"This is a classic case of be careful what you wish for," Hugh whispered in Violet's ear, to which she let out a giggle. She tried to hide her laugh with a cough, but it was too late, the sheriff noticed. He pointed for Jennifer to sit down then turned his attention back to Violet and Hugh.

"Deep Dish and the Professor," he drawled. "You see something funny? I wouldn't be laughing if I were you." He took in the cocktail-strewn table and shook his head. "Or celebrating either. Especially you, Maven. Mrs. Vaughn, Dr. Gordon, I understand you might have some information for us. You're comin' with me to the station."

"Now?" said Violet.

"I forgot, you fancy people need an engraved invitation. Would you be so kind to accompany me to the station," the sheriff said, in a mocking voice.

Hugh looked at Violet. "We might as well get this over with."

Violet and Hugh spent the next hour in the tiny Sheriff's Office, describing their encounter with Bailey, Mateo, Red and Dewer. He asked them in several different ways what time they arrived and left the hot springs and who and what they saw.

"You're lucky someone saw you leaving the area while Dewer was still alive or you'd be my prime suspects—again," he told them. "But I don't think you're telling me the whole story. You're covering for your buddy Maven. I do hope that little restaurant of yours is up to code, Deep Dish. It'd be a shame if you couldn't open on time."

"Are you the Coatimundi health inspector, too?" Asked Violet, incredulous.

"I'm just sayin', sometimes things happen when folks aren't honest with the authorities. So you didn't see Maven out at the hot springs?"

"No," said Hugh. "We only saw her at the entrance, with the protestors. What about the other people we saw out there? Any of them had a motive."

"So now you're investigators again, is that it? The two of you trying to play detective, to show me up?"

The sheriff reached into a box and pulled out a plastic bag with something green in it. Maven's cactus hat. "You ever seen this? Maybe you can explain how it ended up out at the hot springs—right next to the Djinn."

CHAPTER 6

The next morning, Violet and Spirit set off for a walk to investigate the equipment sounds from the previous day. Violet pondered the information the sheriff revealed last night. Why was Maven's cactus hat found where Dewer was murdered? If Maven wanted Violet and Hugh's help in clearing her name, they needed to get more information from her as soon as possible. They couldn't be of much help if Maven wasn't completely honest. With Sheriff Winters' thinly veiled threats about Violet's restaurant, she wasn't sure how much poking around she should be doing. But still, if Dewer truly was murdered, there were multiple people out at the hot springs who could be suspects.

The previous day's rain had passed and today looked to be a gorgeous fall morning in the desert. Violet trekked through the sage, rocks and cactus, headed for the boundary of her property. Something skittered across the path in front of her—a horned lizard, or horny toad, as the locals called them. Covered with spikes, he looked like a tiny dinosaur. They were a protected species now, due to their dwindling numbers. These poor creatures will be another casualty of that big new development, she thought, as she watched the little guy run for cover.

She climbed to the top of a small bluff that signaled the end of her property. The source of the noise became evident right away. At the bottom of the slope, several pieces of heavy equipment sat idle with no operators in sight. It appeared they were in the process of cutting a road through the mesa. Ugh, Red Clayton, she thought. He's behind this.

She had an inkling of what he might be planning and the thought filled her with dread. It couldn't be a coincidence the road looked to be heading in the direction of Emerald Eyes. He must have a plan to develop some of the land between here and there. But things were quiet today. The death of Mr. Dewer must have shut down operations for now. She added Red to her list of people to talk to.

She and Spirit wound their way through the brush to the main dirt road. Violet turned for home, but Spirit wouldn't budge. He looked up the road toward Red's place, ears perked up. Then Violet heard it too— a gravelly, scraping sound, coming closer.

The source of the noise came into view. A middle-aged Hispanic woman, laden with bags, moved slowly up the road from the direction of the Clayton Ranch, pulling a suitcase that bounced and scraped on the dirt. Violet waited for the woman to get closer, then held up a hand in greeting. She recognized her from the Clayton ranch.

"Hello there! It's Rosa, isn't it? You work for Red Clayton? Here, come set your things down."

Rosa reached Violet and dropped the bags with a thump. "I *worked* for Mr. Clayton." She sat down on her suitcase, out of breath. Spirit approached her, tail wagging, and she patted his head.

"I see," said Violet. She put two and two together and it equaled Mateo. "Let's get you to my house for something to drink. That's quite a hike from the Clayton place." Violet picked up one of the suitcases and led the way to her trailer.

Inside, she settled her guest and brought her some ice water and a slice of chocolate cake. Maybe not the healthiest breakfast, but Rosa looked in need of emotional support—everyone knows chocolate cake is tonic for the soul.

After a bite, she raised her eyebrows. "Oh! This is…so good. It tastes like Mexican cocoa, but a little different." Rosa spoke with an accent that revealed English was not her native language.

"You have a good palate," said Violet. "Yes, a specialty cocoa from the farmer's market in Albuquerque."

Rosa closed her eyes, enjoying her emotional support cake.

"Do you mind sharing what happened?" Violet prodded.

Rosa set her cake down and clasped her hands together. "My son, Mateo."

Violet nodded. Just as she suspected.

"He's become, well—very close with Mr. Clayton's daughter, Bailey. I knew something was going on. I asked him about it. He denied it. But a mama always knows."

Rosa was now wringing her hands, clearly distressed. "I thought to myself, why not? They grew up together, running all over that ranch. But—I've been so worried."

"Worried about Mr. Clayton finding out?"

"Who, him? No, not about that. Mateo has worked with the animals on the ranch since he was a boy. He wants to go to veterinary school. He's just doing the construction job to save money. I was worried about him getting mixed up with a girl and throwing away his future. I should have put a stop to it. Now, it's too late. Everything's ruined."

The tears rimming Rosa's eyes finally spilled over and ran down her face. Violet found some tissue and handed it to her.

"Mr. Clayton doesn't think my Mateo is good enough for his daughter. And, even worse, he thinks— he thinks Mateo did something terrible. After twenty years of loyal service, this is what I get? So, I quit. Let them cook for themselves. I don't think any of them even know how to turn on the stove."

"I know about Mateo getting fired by Dewer," said Violet. "I was out at the hot springs when it happened. And I know Dewer was found dead."

Rosa's eyes went wide. "You were there? Then you must know Mateo didn't do it. Mr. Clayton is saying my son might have—done something to that man. But knowing Mr. Clayton, he's probably involved in it himself."

An idea was slowly turning around in Violet's

head. "What are your plans? Were you going to walk all the way into town?"

"I have no choice, I don't have a car. Mateo shares a place in town with a bunch of other boys. I'm sure he doesn't want his mama moving in with him. I might ask for a job at the barbecue place. I don't know —" She trailed off, starting to cry again.

Violet moved to sit next to Rosa and put an arm around her shoulder. "It's gonna be alright. I have an idea. Here—" She handed Rosa the slice of cake.

Rosa dabbed her eyes with the tissue then took a bite. "This cake is good. But I don't think it's going to solve all my problems."

"The cake's just to make you feel better. Here's my idea. I'm opening a restaurant in Coatimundi. It started out as a pizza place, but it's evolving into a café that has unique Southwestern food. I've been looking for a cook, but I haven't found the right person. I think you might be perfect."

She could see hope lighting Rosa's eyes. She needed to continue with the whole idea before the woman got too excited.

"The thing is, I can't really pay you until after we open. I'm stretched pretty thin until then. But I can offer you room and board. Here, with me."

Rosa clasped her hands in prayer and bowed her head. Finally, she looked up and met Violet's eyes. "Yes, it sounds perfect. Thank you so much. It's a good plan. We can both help each other. But—you're the lady who solved that crime with the man who lived here, and the money, right? Please, can you help me clear Mateo's name?"

Hugh told Violet he was a serial helper. Now Violet began to think she had the same affliction. With her restaurant opening in a week, her plate was completely full. On top of that, she already agreed to help Maven get off the suspect list. And yet, looking into Rosa's hopeful, tear-filled eyes, she couldn't say no. Besides, she would already be asking some questions on Maven's behalf, what was one more suspect in the mix?

"I'm not sure what I can do, but I'll see what we can find out." She handed Rosa one of the fliers advertising the opening of Deep Dish. "The work starts today. On both fronts. We're going to the Desert Harvest Festival."

CHAPTER 7

Banners for the harvest festival stretched across Main Street. Orange, yellow and red flowers festooned the light polls. Booths lined both sides of the street. Mounds of produce spilled out of market stalls while shoppers and tourists filled their bags and baskets with goods. The air was fragrant with mingled smells from apples to pumpkins to roasting peppers.

Violet and Rosa stopped by Deep Dish first so Rosa could meet Gabriel and check out the sparkling new kitchen.

Upon seeing Rosa, Gabriel burst into a wide grin. "Mrs. Ayala, I know your son, Mateo. We did 4H together. He's amazing with animals, we all thought he'd end up being a vet."

Rosa's brow creased in worry. "He is going to be a vet–if he sticks with the plan."

"Well I'm glad you're joining us. I still remember the tamales you made for our 4H pot luck. They were the best I ever tasted. And now we can stop looking for someone and just focus on the opening night."

"Can I leave Spirit here with you?" Violet asked. The dog was already at Gabriel's side, the two of them having formed an instant friendship.

Gabriel ruffled Spirit's fur. "Of course, he's my right-hand man."

Violet and Rosa headed out to the festival. They agreed to split up to hand out fliers for the new restaurant. They also each had separate tasks. Violet wanted to find Maven to ask a few more questions and Rosa needed to locate Mateo. Besides that, Violet hoped to check out the local farm offerings. She might be able to source ingredients from some of them. Also on her list was to find a gift for Hugh's daughter, Bella.

She tried to stick to her mission of giving flyers to everyone she could, but she kept getting distracted by the lovely fall displays. The baskets in one colorful booth overflowed with a variety of squash, most of which Violet had never seen before. She looked through the bins, finding squashes in bright orange, yellow, green and even purple, some warty, some smooth. She got contact info from the vendor, her head already filling with ideas on how to use the colorful vegetables.

She began to notice that most people were wearing one of two buttons. Some were light blue with a cactus in the middle and read, "Vote for a Better Tamara." The competing buttons said simply, "Vote RED." Looks like the mayoral candidates are taking advantage of the festival, she thought. It would be a good opportunity to ask both of them some questions, as both were at Emerald Eyes the day Dewer was killed.

She passed a booth that exuded the delicious aroma of roasting chilies. A large grill smoked and sizzled, manned by none other than Dr. Pepper, her friend from the Navajo Nation and the king of all peppers in the region.

He gave her a wave and a smile. "I was hoping to see you. My nephew told me you want some of the Big Jims. I've got a case set aside." He had to shout over the din of the festival. "Will you be in White Feather soon?"

"I think Hugh said something about going tomorrow. I have some other things to get there too. Maybe I'll tag along. I know the restaurant's in good hands with Gabriel. He's an exceptional young man, you should be proud."

Dr. Pepper beamed. "I'm glad to know he's working out." He gave a wave then went back to his grill work.

She noticed a large crowd gathered around a booth with a red awning. A sign proclaimed "Free hot dogs and cokes!" Red Clayton stood in front, glad handing and chatting with the locals, while workers gave out food. There was a tap on Violet's shoulder and she spun around to see Dr. Kai Wauneka, the veterinarian who had given her the hat.

"You here for the free hot dogs?" he said jokingly.

"As if. I don't need anything from Red Clayton. I want to find Tamara and get one of her buttons."

He reached into his pocket and pulled out one of the light blue buttons. "She deputized me." He pointed to the "Better Tamara" badge on his chest. "You coming with Hugh tomorrow? Grace would love to see you."

Kai and Grace Wauneka's sister, Rainy, was one of three murder victims in the small town of White Feather in the Navajo Nation. As a forensic psychologist, Hugh had taken an interest in the crimes as well as the lack of attention they received. His reason for staying in Coatimundi was to write a book about the murders.

Before Violet could answer, a commotion near Red's booth took her attention.

Dr. Tamara Goodwill stood in front of the booth, staring him down. She wore a long, loose skirt, cowboy boots and a T-shirt with the "Vote for a Better Tamara" slogan.

"Take a good look at this, folks," she said, pointing to Red's booth. "He's giving out free hot dogs with one hand and destroying our desert with the other. Those hot dogs come with a price."

Some people began to move away from Red's booth and a few actually set their hot dogs back down.

"I'm gonna give you something free, too," she continued. "The freedom to roam our beautiful desert landscape without big developments, traffic and pollution."

Applause broke out. The crowd from Red's booth were now flocking to Tamara for buttons and flyers. Red Clayton's face burned with his namesake color. Violet decided today was not the day to ask questions of either mayoral candidate, as both seemed to have their hands full.

Behind Kai's shoulder, Violet saw Rosa pushing her way through the crowd, her son Mateo in tow. Violet waved her over and made introductions to Kai.

Kai patted Mateo's shoulder. "I know this one. He's got a heckuva way with animals. How's our little lamb doing, the one that wouldn't nurse?"

Mateo shuffled his feet. "I'm not working out there anymore, sir. I was—"

Rosa stepped up. "He was fired, that's what. By him." She pointed over to Red's booth. "And fired from his construction job too, by that—that Dewer man."

Mateo made a stop sign with his hand. "Mom, please—"

"No, Mateo. I stood by long enough. I'm not going to let my son's future be ruined. That's why you need to talk to Mrs. Vaughn. She's investigating the murder of that Dewer man."

"I wouldn't say investigating," said Violet, wishing she had never agreed to help anyone and could just go on and enjoy the harvest day. "I'm just—trying to help out a friend," she finished, weakly.

Kai followed the whole exchange with an amused look on his face. "So, the detective's back at it."

Violet shook her head. "Let's not let that get around."

"Tell you what," Kai said to Mateo. "Come to my office in White Feather tomorrow. I could use someone who's good with large animals."

Mateo's face lit up with sheer joy. "Really? Yes, sir, I will. Thank you!"

Kai headed off to check out the festival and Violet guided Rosa and Mateo to a nearby bench.

Violet got right to the point, wanting to get back to the festival herself. "I just wanted to hear from you, Mateo. What happened at the hot springs after you stormed off? Where did you go?"

"I already told all that to the sheriff," he said.

His mom poked him in the ribs. "Tell it again. She's trying to help us. Tell her everything." She nodded her head to punctuate the statement and Mateo straightened up.

"After Mr. Dewer fired me, I stormed off, like you said. I walked around the hot springs and across the valley. You know how the area is surrounded with those tall cliffs? They're full of caves, and there's one where Bailey and I always go. I went there and just cooled off for awhile and finally Bailey came and found me."

"Did you see anyone else out at the hot springs?" Violet asked.

"Yeah. I saw the two ladies. Out near the Djinn."

"Two ladies?" said Violet. "Who were they? Did you recognize them?"

Mateo looked straight ahead to where shoppers milled about. "It was—them," he said, pointing.

Violet's gaze followed his finger and landed on two women who stood side by side, heads bent together in whispered discussion.

Maven. And Dr. Tamara Goodwill.

CHAPTER 8

Violet made quick goodbyes to Rosa and Mateo. "Catch up with you later!" she called over her shoulder.

She approached Maven and Tamara who stood with heads bent together in the middle of the crowded walkway. Maven held a clipboard in her hands and a stack of her own printed leaflets.

Tamara looked up and smiled at Violet. "Hey there! How's that head wound?"

Violet took off her cowboy hat to show her hair, now completely grown back. She had been under the doctor's care a few months ago when she was attacked.

"It's all good now," said Violet. "Hey doctor, since I've got you here—"

Someone up the road called Tamara's name and she waved. "I've gotta get back on the campaign trail," she said. Then she looked at Maven and made a muscle with her arm. "Stay strong." She walked away, nodding and waving at the townsfolk. Violet almost called her back but then had second thoughts. It might be better to talk to Maven alone.

"I've been looking for you," she said to Maven.

"How are you holding up?"

Maven shook her head, looking uncharacteristically morose. "It's just not right."

"Well, I'm already talking to people who were out there and trying to figure out what happened. I have some questions for you, too."

"Wait. What in the desert dung are you talkin' about?" Maven's face scrunched up in confusion.

"Dewer's murder. You know, the one the sheriff suspects you of?"

"Oh that." Maven made a phfft sound. "I'm not worried about that. It'll all get sorted out."

"Maddie's worried about it. You should be, too. Sheriff Winters is no joke. What were *you* talking about?"

"The development, of course. It's paused for now. But word is Clayton's gonna move forward." Her turquoise bracelets jangled as she waved a flyer at Violet. "This spells it all out."

"Okay. Back to the murder though. Last night, the sheriff said they found your hat near the Djinn. And another witness says you were out there with Tamara. So—were you?"

Maven looked around at the people passing by. She pulled Violet along with her and into a little alley between two buildings.

"Okay," Maven said. "I was out there. But it's not what you think."

"I don't think you did anything to Dewer. It's what the sheriff thinks that matters."

"After the protest wound down, I decided I

wanted some pictures of the Mesa Verde cactus for my brochures. I went on out there and was just minding my own business when I came across Dewer. He was over near the Djinn, taking pictures himself—of the railings and such. He was stomping around on the ground, like testing it out. I decided to give him a piece of my mind."

Violet began to get nervous where this story was going. She almost didn't want to hear it, but she had to ask. "What happened?"

"I lay into him, telling him he wasn't gonna get away with trashing Emerald Eyes. He said he didn't care what I thought and it's a done deal. I was mad, I tell you what. I threw my hat at him and I left. I ran into Tamara as I walked back to my truck. She was worried I'd been gone so long."

"Did Tamara see you with Dewer? And did you see anyone else?"

"She says she never saw Dewer. We only saw one other person out there."

Violet leaned in eagerly. "Really? Who?"

"Red's kid. Bailey Clayton."

Violet pursed her lips and whispered a long, slow, "Ohh." The more questions she asked, the more curious things became.

Violet made her way along Main Street, handing flyers out to people and looking at the booths. Her mind spun with information. Who knew Emerald Eyes Hot Springs was such a hotbed of drama? She was anxious to talk everything over with Hugh and hear his perspective. She found that when he wasn't around, she missed him. The unfamiliar sensation felt both wonderful and scary.

She came upon a booth selling little cacti in hand-painted pots. They would make a perfect gift for Bella.

"I can put together a gift basket for you," said the vendor, a tiny, elderly woman in an enormous straw hat. "With some prickly pear gummy bears, those are popular. Here, try one."

Violet picked up one of the bright pink gummies. "It tastes like—watermelon. No, bubble gum!"

The vendor smiled broadly. "Most people are surprised how good they are. Prickly pear has an amazing, sweet flavor. It's perfect for candies. We have jelly, too."

Violet purchased the gifts, then ambled up the road. She had given out all her flyers and felt encouraged by the number of people who called out, "When's that restaurant of yours gonna open?" She needed to find Rosa and head over to Deep Dish to finish some work.

She heard her name called and turned to see Hugh making his way through the crowd alongside a pretty girl in her late teens. Violet had seen pictures of Hugh's daughter, but in real life the young woman looked like a fairy princess, with delicate features and long blond hair. Hugh gave a hearty wave and hurried to meet Violet.

"This is my daughter, Bella," said Hugh,

beaming. Then he placed an arm around Violet's shoulder. "And this is the woman I've been telling you about. Violet Vaughn."

Was he blushing, Violet wondered. He looked nervous and scattered, as if he was introducing his prom date to his parents.

Violet stretched out her hand. "Hello! I'm so happy to finally meet you, Bella."

Bella barely touched Violet's hand, looking like Hugh had just introduced his good friend, the serial killer. "Oh. Hello," she managed.

She's probably just overwhelmed, Violet thought. She held out the gift basket. "Here's a little taste of the Southwest for you, to welcome you to Coatimundi."

Bella took the basket and peered inside. "A cactus? That should be handy for my flight home. And —what are these? Cactus candy?" Although her British accent had an air of politeness, the words were all sarcasm.

"They're prickly pear gummy bears," Violet put in hastily, "I just tried them, they're delicious."

"Oh," Bella said dryly. "Yummy."

"I think Bella's a wee bit tired," Hugh put in, "We're gonna head to Maven's Haven to get her settled."

Violet, stung and disappointed, just nodded.

"Bella's doing a hike tomorrow, but I'm heading to White Feather," said Hugh, "You joining me?"

Violet nodded again, still unable to speak.

"Great," he said, "Pick you up at nine."

Violet watched father and daughter head up the street. Bella now looked animated, hugging her dad and chatting. Doesn't look a wee bit tired to me, Violet thought.

Hours later, Violet and Rosa worked side by side, polishing every table in the restaurant while Gabriel got the afternoon off to spend time at the harvest festival. Whenever Spirit was at Deep Dish, he spent his time gazing out the front window and guarding the front door. Like all border collies, he needed a job to do, and he took the role seriously, ears perked up and eyes scanning.

"She looked at me like I was pond scum," said Violet. "And Hugh didn't say a word." During their cleaning, Violet told the whole story of her relationship with Hugh, beginning with meeting in an RV park and ending with Bella. Violet found Rosa very easy to talk to and it hadn't taken long to start spilling her guts about what was foremost on her mind.

Rosa paused in her vigorous polishing of a tabletop. "The girl, all she knows is, her parents got divorced and her dad ran off to the desert with some lady whose husband was murdered. Give it some time. But with kids that age, I tell you this—don't show your cards. You know? Don't let her see she's getting to you. As for the dad, that's easy. He's blind to his little girl's faults."

Violet was processing Rosa's advice when Spirit

let out a low growl. The restaurant door opened and a man peered in. Not just any man. Maybe the most handsome man Violet had ever seen. He was very tall, with dark hair that showed a little gray at the sides. He wore horn-rim glasses that might have made any other man look dorky, but on him looked somehow nerdy-sexy.

"Wow," Violet whispered. Then she shook her head a little bit, realizing she said it out loud. She cleared her throat. "Wow, I thought we had that door locked. Um—what can I do for you?"

"Hi there," the man said in a deep voice. "We just wanted to check to see if you were open yet. Looks like we're out of luck." By this point, he had stepped into the restaurant, followed by another man, who was of slight build, balding, also with glasses, although not quite the nerdy sexy vibe as his friend. Spirit pointed his nose toward the second man and sniffed. He didn't drop his alert stance.

"We'll be open next week, said Violet, moving forward to give the handsome man a flier. "There's a coupon on here for buy one get one." She felt like a babbling idiot. Rosa continued her polishing, following the exchange with her eyes.

The second man backed away from Spirit. "You shouldn't have that dog in a restaurant. It's not sanitary."

"He's just here while we prepare for the opening," said Violet. She called Spirit and he reluctantly trotted to her side, still eyeing the men.

The handsome man shot an annoyed look at

his friend. "I'm Kent and this is Fritz. We work up at Coati Peak, the stellar observatory. We've been excited for a new place to eat when we come into town."

"The observatory, that's interesting," said Violet. "Can't you just get your meals beamed up from the aliens?"

The grumpy Fritz rolled his eyes, an exasperated look on his face. "You should watch a few episodes of Star Trek before you go throwing around incorrect references."

"Oh, was that from Star Trek?" Violet laughed. "Star Wars, Star Trek, I don't know, I get them mixed up."

"I'll just—wait outside," said Fritz. He actually looked like he was ready to commit murder over a sci-fi blunder.

"I was just teasing," Violet said, after he left. "I'm a huge Star Trek fan. Whenever I'm down, I binge-watch episodes of Next Gen."

"Sorry about Fritz," said Kent. "He spends way too much time alone in a lab up on a cliff. He's–socially awkward."

Violet nodded. She couldn't disagree. "Is it true the observatory's not open to the public?"

"I guess you could say it's—by invitation only." He gave Violet a shy smile that made her have to mentally slap herself and remember Hugh. She and Hugh had an understanding—didn't they? But she wasn't dead, either.

"But—I might be willing to trade a tour for a buy one get one free coupon. Is this your phone number on the flier?"

Violet nodded.

"I'll give you a call to arrange a tour. Now, I guess it's off to Badlands for barbecue again."

Violet went back to polishing tables and noticed Rosa looking at her disapprovingly, making some kind of mmm mmm sound with pursed lips and shaking her head.

"What?" said Violet, feeling her cheeks start to burn. "I'm just being friendly. We need the business."

"Oh, that's what it was?" said Rosa, with a smile. "Okay. But I'm gonna keep my eye on that one. There's something I don't like about him—and his little friend."

Spirit watched through the window in the direction the men left until long after they were gone.

CHAPTER 9

"So, we have Mateo, Bailey, Maven and Tamara, all wandering around the hot springs at the same time as Dewer." Violet sat in the passenger seat of Hugh's car, headed toward White Feather. She held up a finger with each name as she ticked them off.

"Those hot springs are a boiling bowl of suspect soup," said Hugh. "But you forgot one key ingredient—Red Clayton."

Violet chuckled. "I think Red would make the soup too bitter. But you're right—" She held up a fifth finger. "He's also in the suspect soup."

"You would probably throw some hatch chilies in there and put it on the menu at Deep Dish."

Violet poked him playfully in the arm. "Are you making fun of my pepper obsession?"

"Never," he said, with mock seriousness.

Violet looked at Hugh's profile as he drove. Over the past few months, it seemed obstacles and misunderstandings had prevented them from taking their relationship to the next level. Hugh's divorce had only recently been finalized. Between his book and her restaurant, their time together had been limited. She wondered now if the distance that remained between them was mostly her fault. After her abusive marriage, she tended to keep men at arm's length. Hugh was such a gentleman—maybe too much so.

"What do you want to do while I'm interviewing the family?" he asked, interrupting her thoughts. His mission in White Feather today was to visit the parents of one of the young murder victims.

"I'd like to visit Grace and I need to pick up an order from Dr. Pepper—maybe Grace can help me find his place."

Hugh nodded. "Before we get to the Navajo Nation, I need to take a quick detour. Someone contacted me saying they have information about the White Feather murders. I need to meet with him first and see what he's got."

"Did you tell Montoya about it?" Special Agent Montoya from the FBI had been the chief investigator into the crimes committed by Violet's husband, Jim. While in Coatimundi, Montoya learned about the White Feather murders on the Navajo Nation and asked to be assigned to the case. Violet respected the agent's skill, but knew she was not keen on Hugh's decision to write a book about the murders.

"I don't know if there's anything to it, yet," said Hugh. "He contacted me online and said he knew something. He suggested a place to meet between Coatimundi and White Feather."

At that moment, the GPS interrupted with a directive to turn right.

Violet took in the surroundings. Bare desert without a dwelling in sight. Hugh slowed down and they came upon a gravel road without even a signpost.

"You sure this is safe?" she asked.

"I've gotten a bunch of tips and most of them amount to nothing. This is probably somebody's idea of a joke. I put the coordinates into the GPS. Let's follow on a little more and see where we end up."

They drove slowly along the narrow lane, barbed wire fences on each side seemingly fencing off nothing. Brush and sage stretched for miles with the occasional saguaro cactus waving at them. A road runner skittered across their path, the sun glinting off the turquoise blue in his tail.

Eventually, a small structure appeared, some distance off the road. As they drove closer, they saw a beat-up mailbox attached to the fence and a closed, metal gate.

"You have arrived at your destination," said the GPS.

"Really?" said Violet, giving the GPS a side-eye.

Beyond the gate, a straight, narrow dirt drive led across an acre of brush to a boarded-up, ramshackle dwelling.

"This looks a little dodgy," said Hugh. "I think someone's pulling my leg."

"Just a *little* dodgy? It looks like something from a horror movie. What time was the person going to meet you here?"

"Ten o'clock." Hugh looked at his watch. "We have a couple of minutes. But I expect it's just a prank."

"Let's walk up to the house—if you can call it a house—and get some pictures. I want to send Maven and Maddie shots of us in front of a haunted shack. That'll crack them up."

They pushed on the gate and it swung open with a loud, rusty screech.

"It looks like rattlesnake city," said Hugh. "We need Spirit."

Violet decided to leave Spirit at Deep Dish to keep Rosa company while she worked.

"He's my chief snake alarm," Violet agreed. "And he just had his rattlesnake vaccine, so I'm not as worried about him now."

They walked up the rutted dirt drive toward the shack, passing a heap of rubble mounded with chunks of cement and rebar. The barbed wire fence surrounding the property was piled with tumbleweeds and the occasional stack of old tires.

The shack itself leaned significantly, as if the sun was melting it into the earth. The flat-roofed dwelling might have originally been plain white, but was now a patchwork of old boards, scavenged metal and plywood. Some rusty barrels lay on their sides near the front door, completing the creepy look.

Violet and Hugh took turns posing for pictures in front of the shack. Then Hugh pulled her in close for a selfie.

After the picture, Hugh continued to hold her. "This is nice," he said, close to her ear.

Violet felt a melting inside and relaxed into Hugh's embrace.

Then, she heard a noise. A far off buzzing sound. "You hear that?" she asked.

"I think it's my heartbeat," said Hugh, his eyes a little glazed over.

"No, listen." Sure enough, the sound was coming closer.

"It sounds like a motorcycle or—a dirt bike," he said, putting his hand up to shade his eyes. "Maybe my tipster will show up after all."

A cyclist came into view, screaming down the road at breakneck speed, dust flying out behind the bike. As it came closer, they saw a black dirt bike with a rider dressed in dark clothing. His head and face were obscured by a shiny black helmet with a tinted visor. The rider slowed when he approached the gate, rolling through and coming to a stop.

Hugh gave a friendly wave as he and Violet began to walk toward the gate. The masked rider did not wave back. He revved his bike and began driving right toward them. There was something in his hand and he began to raise it in the air. A baseball bat.

"Run!" Hugh cried, but the fast-moving cyclist was already close. He swung the bat at Hugh who leapt out of the way just in time, rolling in the dirt near the pile of rubble. Violet ran to help Hugh, but again, he yelled, "Run, Violet!"

Hugh pushed himself up and pulled a piece of rebar out of the rubble. Violet looked around frantically for a weapon. She picked up a fist-sized rock and looked for the rider. He had swung around in front of the shack and was moving toward them again, bat in hand. Violet threw her rock. It missed. The rider drove straight toward Hugh, but Hugh stood his ground. When the bike got close, Hugh took a swing with the rebar and landed a blow on the cyclist's arm. The bike wobbled and skidded out in the dirt. The masked rider pushed himself up and abandoned the bike. He walked menacingly toward Hugh, still holding the bat.

Pure terror filled Violet. She felt helpless and looked desperately for more rocks. "What do you want with us?" she screamed. "Leave us alone!"

Then Hugh did something odd. He curved his left arm up over his head and bent his knees. He held the rebar out in front of him, like a sword.

"En garde, you little twit," he called.

The masked man swooped the bat in front of him, trying to club Hugh in the side. But Hugh artfully stepped out of the way. He thrust with the metal rod, landing a stab to the intruder's ribs that sent him stumbling back.

Again, the man in black came at Hugh, this time swinging the bat with both hands. Hugh parried the swing and then redirected the rebar, poking the man in the neck.

The breath was knocked out of the man and he dropped the bat. He turned and ran, picking up his bike, jumping on and starting it in a flurry. Violet thought to open the camera on her phone and snapped a few shots as the rider drove away.

Then she looked over at Hugh. He was slightly out of breath, but he raised the metal rod toward her in a salute. "Four years fencing at uni. Team captain."

Violet ran to him and they hugged tight. "What

—what was that?" she said, her voice shaking.

"I'd call that a warning," said Hugh. "That might have been the White Feather killer himself."

CHAPTER 10

Violet sat on Grace Wauneka's couch, a mug of hot tea in one hand and a large chunk of pumpkin bread in the other. Grace was obviously a kindred spirit. She knew emotional support came in the form of carbs. Under the glare of Special Agent Montoya, Violet tried to shrink into the sofa. She stuffed a piece of the soft and spicy bread in her mouth.

"What were you thinking?" Montoya put her hands on her hips and held her head up to the sky in exasperation. "No, forget it, don't tell me. I should know by now that you two think rules don't apply to you. Despite almost getting killed a few months ago, you're gonna go out in the desert to meet someone off the internet? We're talking about a murderer here. You should know better, Dr. Gordon."

"Point taken," said Hugh, looking sufficiently chastised. "But—I think our little escapade might turn into a break in the case. Violet has a few pictures and you can track the email I received."

"Yeah, my team's already on it. But I'm not willing to sacrifice lives in this pursuit, especially civilians—even nosy ones."

Montoya exited the room, closely followed by

Kai Wauneka, still mooning after the agent, judging from his rapt expression. Hugh followed after him, explaining he needed to go meet the family for his interview.

Now alone with Grace, Violet took a drink of the tea. She couldn't place the flavor, but it had a fresh, green and grassy taste.

"You like my Navajo Tea?" asked Grace, as if reading her mind.

Violet took another sip. "Yes, it's very soothing. Just what I need right now. What kind of tea is it?"

"It's becoming a lost art. It's made from the greenthread plant. I used to go and gather it with my grandmother—Rainy and I did."

"You must miss your sister," said Violet.

Grace nodded sadly. "She loved all the traditional stuff. She used to help with buying merchandise for the Trading Post. She'd find local artists and craftsmen. Then she decided she wanted to go to law school to help people here in White Feather."

Violet was still reeling from the encounter with the masked biker. If he was the White Feather killer, she shuddered to think about the innocent, young Rainy in his hands. She didn't want Grace's thoughts to go there.

"I think my nerves are finally starting to calm down," Violet said, setting her mug on the coffee table. "I need to pick up an order from Dr. Pepper. It will be awhile until Hugh finishes his interview. Can you give me a lift?"

"Sure. But I have to run into the Trading Post.

I'm training a new clerk and I need to check on her."

Inside Grace's store, Violet once again marveled at the vast display of goods and works of art. She looked down at her feet to admire the boots Hugh bought here, the leather now pleasingly worn and the fit like a second skin. Just like last time, she couldn't afford much, her finances stretched to the limit on the restaurant. The clerk, a girl of eighteen or nineteen, appeared to be taking the job seriously and Grace was satisfied, so they headed out to Dr. Pepper's place.

As Grace drove, Violet took in the sights of White Feather. Small, flat-roofed houses lined the streets, identical in size and shape, but each with its own personality. Some folks sat out on their porches and every one of them waved at Grace as they passed. Convenience stores and fast-food places pushed their way into the landscape, their bright, flashy signs somehow out of sync with the serene desert vistas.

"I really enjoyed your tea and bread," Violet said. "Do most people around here eat traditional foods?"

"Unfortunately, no. That's why I said it's a lost art. If you look around, you see there's lots of poverty here. This county is one of the poorest in the entire country. Fast food and junk food are cheap. But a lot of people want to get away from that. Actually, I just started teaching a class on traditional foods at the community college. I got so many sign-ups, we have to open up another class."

"I'd love to sit in on one of your classes," said Violet. "So how did you become so knowledgeable on

Navajo cooking?"

"I'm not really an expert. I grew up eating a lot of junk, too. But we lost both our parents to diabetes. And then, we lost Rainy. After that, I decided to make some changes. I started talking to some of the older people in the community and remembering things my grandmother taught me, like the tea. It's been my —therapy, I guess you'd say."

"I'm well-acquainted with food as therapy," said Violet, "It's my specialty."

"Here's Pep's place," said Grace, slowing the truck. If food is therapy, then he has a PhD."

"He is Dr. Pepper, after all," said Violet, stepping out of the truck.

She was met with a rich, spicy smell. Not roasting peppers, but the deeper scent of ground spice. The source of the aroma became clear as they approached the covered patio adjacent to Pep's house. Large bundles of peppers hung from the rafters, drying. Two women sat at a long table, filling jars with a deep-red powder. Dr. Pepper loaded crates into the back of a pickup. When he saw them, he paused in his work and retrieved another crate from a stack and set it on the table.

"Here's your Big Jims," he said. "These are some beauties. I guess it was a good year."

Violet could see the shiny emerald green and red peppers through the holes in the box.

"Thank you," she said, "But right now I'm intrigued by this other operation." She pointed to the jars. "Chile powder?"

"Yes. Our own blend."

Pep introduced his mother and his wife and then gave Violet and Grace a sample of the ground spice. One taste was all it took for Violet to know it was something special. It could be incorporated into so many different Southwestern recipes. She bought a jar and arranged for more in a few weeks.

"How's Obi Wan?" Pep asked, using his nickname for Hugh. "Has he made any progress finding the killer?"

Violet described the harrowing encounter from that morning. She could see the fear in the eyes of Pep's mother and wife. In a town this small, the loss of three women affected everyone. Three women that they knew of, who knew how many more. The terror wasn't going away until someone was caught, Violet thought grimly.

On the drive back to Coatimundi, Hugh's lips were drawn in a tight line, his usual lighthearted banter missing.

"How did things go with the interview?" Violet ventured.

He blew out a long breath. "The parents I talked to today, Mirage Yazzi's family—they're completely destroyed. They'll never be the same. I started out wanting to write a book. Now, I just want to get this guy. And I'm also kicking myself for earlier today. I put you in danger."

Violet put a hand on his shoulder. "What's that you told me a few months ago? There are no victims, only volunteers? Well, I volunteered to go with you. We've been through some scrapes before, and knowing us, we'll be in some again. I know what I'm getting into. And speaking of scrapes, I keep thinking about Maven."

"I'm worried, too," said Hugh. "She was at the scene of the crime and she had a beef with Dewer."

Violet nodded. "I don't think she did it, but it doesn't look good."

"Dewer was a pretty big guy," said Hugh. "I don't think Maven could force him over the side of the Djinn."

"Anyone could have pushed him if they snuck up on him while he was taking pictures. Even Bailey Clayton."

They rode in silence for the rest of the journey. Violet felt the weight of the day's events and she was sure Hugh felt the same. By the time they pulled up at her trailer, she realized she was starving.

"You want to come in for some dinner?" she asked.

"I need to get back to Bella. But thanks." He gave her hand a squeeze and she stepped out of the car. Then she poked her head back through the window.

"Hey, you know my opening is on Halloween night. I just wanted to make sure you'll be there."

A funny look crossed Hugh's face, an expression Violet couldn't interpret, but she knew it wasn't good.

"You're asking me if I'm coming to your opening? Really?" He shook his head. "I just don't get you sometimes, Violet. Do you think I would miss that? I mean—what are we doing here? I'll—I'll see you later."

He started to drive off. "Wait—Hugh!" she called. But he kept going.

Dust flew off the blue mini bouncing down the rutted road toward town. Violet stood in her drive and saw ominous, dark thunderclouds rolling in. A great emptiness filled her. More than that, a feeling she might have seriously messed up and hurt Hugh's feelings.

Then she heard a bark and turned to see Spirit running toward her at full speed, Rosa trailing behind him. At least someone was happy with her. She knelt down to greet the swirling, jumping, tail-wagging dog, hugging him even tighter than usual. Then she stood up and put a hand to her chest where Hugh's exit had left a painful sting. She met Rosa's eyes and saw recognition there.

"Love?" Rosa asked.

"Is that what it is?"

Rosa nodded. She set a hand lightly on Violet's shoulder. "Come. I made you something."

Violet let out a long breath. "Oh please let it be food."

CHAPTER 11

"Oh my gosh, what is this?" Violet looked at the packet that Rosa placed in front of her. It looked like a giant wrapped candy. The fist-sized ball, covered in corn leaves and tied at each end with twine, emitted a delicious, spicy aroma.

"Chanchames," she said. "From Yucatan, where my family comes from. It's a kind of tamale. I'm trying my own version for you to maybe put at the restaurant. This one is corn masa, filled with pork, hatch chile, cheese and pumpkin seeds."

Violet savored Rosa's creation and felt her worries begin to melt away. "I bet Red Clayton is kicking himself right now for letting you get away."

Rosa chuckled. "He does love my cooking."

"You said you wouldn't be surprised if he were involved in Dewer's death. What made you say that?"

Rosa shook her head. "He's so secretive about his business things, especially lately. And I heard him saying he wasn't happy with that Dewer man. I don't know. I just know he shouldn't be bringing my son into this. It's all because he doesn't want Mateo seeing Bailey. None of this would have happened if Mrs. Clayton were here."

"Mrs. Clayton?" Violet stopped mid-bite. "He mentioned her when I went out to his house a few months ago, I've been wondering. Where is she?"

Rosa brought them both some coffee and sat down opposite Violet. "She left about a year ago. They were fighting all the time. But, she's a good lady. She doesn't like the way he does business and he doesn't like her getting involved in the ranch. I think she's in New York, where her parents live."

"Can't say I blame her," said Violet. "I wouldn't want to live with Red Clayton. I just know he had something to do with Dewer and who knows what else. I wish I could get into that house to look around."

Rosa peered at Violet over her coffee mug. "Maybe you can."

Violet was beginning to find Rosa had an adventurous side—and she liked it. "What do you mean?"

"What day is it?" said Rosa. "I'm losing track of time lately with everything going on."

"It's Wednesday."

Rosa set her mug down. "Then we have to go tonight."

"Wait—what? What do mean? And what do you mean we?"

"Wednesday was my night off from cooking dinner. They all go into Albuquerque to Mr. Clayton's club. The house is usually empty. And—" She reached into her purse on the bench. "I still have my key."

Violet's brain began to tingle with both possibility and warning. "Wow. I don't know. I've already had one close call today. I don't want to push my luck. Although—" She trailed off, thinking of the wealth of information she might be able to glean from her nefarious neighbor. "Maven is not serious enough about trying to clear her name. She's so wrapped up in stopping the housing project. I'm worried that I'm running out of time to help her."

"And I'm worried about Mateo being blamed for it," said Rosa, "Especially if Mr. Clayton wants to keep him away from Bailey. I know that house better than anybody. I can get us in and out quickly. And anyway, I left my favorite cooking spoons there, I need to go back for those."

A flash of lightning shone through the window, followed moments later by a loud crack of thunder that made both Violet and Rosa jump. Spirit scrambled under the table to lean against Violet's leg.

"I don't know if this is the best weather to be snooping in," said Violet, peering out the dining room window nervously.

"This may be our only chance," said Rosa. "And it might work in our favor. The ranch hands will be indoors. I know where we can park, behind one of the barns where no one will see us."

Violet thought for a moment. She could sit around here and think about Hugh or go with Rosa and maybe find some evidence to clear Maven and Mateo. She got up from the table and found the natural dog sedative Kai gave her. Spirit was a mess during thunder storms. After a dose of this stuff, he would sleep for hours.

"Okay," she said finally. "Let's do it."

Violet stood in the shadows of some potted plants on the enclosed patio at the Clayton mansion. This was the way she and Hugh entered the last time they visited the ranch. Lightning flashed and lit up the courtyard, turning the fountain and statues from pleasant to evil-looking.

Rosa was right. They hadn't seen a soul on their drive in, the barn doors closed tight, the ranch hands in their bunk houses or out for a night in town.

Violet strained to see into the darkness behind the French doors. Suddenly, a black-clad figure appeared through the panes. Her heart jumped into her throat and she let out a little squeal. Then she realized it was Rosa, unlocking the door. Which she should have been expecting, since that was part of the plan they laid out. She just wasn't cut out for this sneaky stuff. Violet was already regretting the mission and told herself if she got out of this unscathed, she would never do it again. Well, she would try anyway.

She slipped through the door and found herself in the same spacious and artfully-decorated den she had been in before. A light shone at the end of a passageway that looked like it led to the kitchen. It gave enough light in the den for them to see without flashlights.

Violet wore the only black she had—dark yoga pants and a Styx T shirt. Rosa wore a black housekeeping apron over dark pants and looked, for all intents and purposes, as if she were coming to clean the house, not burgle it.

"His office is this way," Rosa whispered, pointing in the other direction from the kitchen. Violet followed her, walking past the fireplace and the enormous painting of Kokopelli above the mantel. The dancing figure seemed to stare down at her with disapproval. The last time she was here, Red told her many Native American symbols are full of duality— that with the light comes darkness. Right now, she was feeling the darkness coming off the painting. She hurried to follow Rosa.

They needed their phone flashlights in Red's study. Violet could make out more Native American works of art on the walls. Pottery and other sculptures were artfully placed around the room. The office smelled of leather and wood with the citrusy scent of furniture polish. Violet wondered how someone who obviously had great appreciation for Native American art could have gone so far astray in wanting to trash local landmarks like Emerald Eyes.

Rosa tried a few of the file cabinets, but they were locked. Violet perused the paperwork on top of his desk. She wasn't sure what they were looking for, but felt she would know it when she saw it. The top desk drawer only contained one item--a folded letter. She took it out, shined her flashlight on it and read:

"Dear Red. I'm leaving. I can't take another day of it. You act like you own everything. It was my family money that saved this place when your daddy ran it into the ground. You're happy to take those fat checks from my trust fund, but you can't let me into the decision-making? We could have had a peaceful life out here, just raising sheep and enjoying our blessings. But you're always on to some new scheme. Nothing's ever good enough for you, Red. I'm leaving for awhile to think about what I want to do. Brody and Bailey are busy with their own lives now. Be sure to pay the staff and ranch hands on time. I left cash in the safe for you to give them bonuses on the holidays. Katie."

Violet was so absorbed in the letter, she forgot where she was for a moment. She heard Rosa moving around and snapped out of it. She took a quick picture with her phone and put the letter back in the drawer.

So, Mrs. Clayton's money was—perhaps unknowingly—financing Red's little schemes. That was interesting. She found nothing else in the desk. Rosa shrugged her shoulders and shook her head to show she hadn't found anything either. Then Rosa bent down and took a piece of crumpled legal paper out of the trash. She read a little and then brought it over to Violet.

"This might be something," she whispered.

It looked to be a partial draft of a letter. There were only a few lines, as if the writer had started, changed their mind and thrown it away. Violet scanned the words quickly, feeling the need to get out of there before they pressed their luck too far. She read, "Dewer—things are getting out of control. I just looked at the new plans. If you go through with this, I'm going to lose everything. It's not what we agreed on and I'm tempted to—"

That was all. The letter cut off in mid-sentence. Violet snapped a picture of it, balled it up and replaced it in the trash. She didn't want to remove anything from the place. Snooping was bad enough.

"Let's get out of here," she whispered to Rosa, who nodded in agreement. Just as they came into the den, Violet heard a noise and froze. Two figures were entering through the French doors and she and Rosa had no time to go back to the office without being seen. Violet dropped behind one of the big leather sofas and Rosa crouched down next to her.

"You positive your dad's not home?" a male voice said.

Violet and Rosa looked at each other, eyes wide with recognition. Mateo.

"He's at his club, I told you. Come on, let's go to my room." Anger crossed Rosa's face, and she started to rise up. Violet grabbed her arm, pulling her back down.

"No, Bailey. Stop. We need to talk."

"I don't want to keep talking about it."

Violet couldn't see Bailey, but she imagined the girl with arms crossed and a pout, which seemed to be her standard stance.

"We have to tell somebody," said Mateo, his voice raised. "Right now I'm a suspect, and I didn't even do anything."

"Shh! No. We can't."

"The sheriff came and questioned me again. So you're choosing your dad over me."

"No, they're looking at Maven. My brother told me she's the prime suspect."

"And that's okay? Dang, girl, you're not who I thought you were."

Lightning cracked and lit up the den, bathing the crouching Violet and Rosa in white blue light. From where Violet was positioned, she caught a glare from Kokopelli staring down at her. He knew what Violet felt in her bones—she shouldn't be here.

"You're being so lame," said Bailey. "It's just complicated. We—"

She was cut off as the French doors sounded, yet again.

"My Dad!" Bailey whispered. "Here—hide."

Violet didn't know where the two concealed themselves. All she knew was when Red Clayton walked into his den, four people were crouched and hiding, all under the watchful glare of Kokopelli.

After his footsteps sounded on the tile entry, he stopped.

"Hello?"

Oh man, he senses something, thought Violet, or he heard something.

In one move, Rosa stood up and moved into the den.

"It's just me, Mr. Clayton."

"Oh Rosa, you're back! Thank God," Red gushed. "I'm so hungry. You should see the crap they tried to feed me at the club. I don't know what it was, but all I've eaten since you've left is cereal."

"I'm not back to stay, Mr. Clayton. I just came

back for my spoons. But—" she paused dramatically. "I guess I could cook you something quick, like an omelette."

"Oh that sounds good, your omelettes are the best."

Violet heard their voices trailing away toward the kitchen. She knew Rosa didn't want to cook another meal for Clayton. She was making the sacrifice so Violet and Mateo could get out of there.

"Why's your mom here?" she heard Bailey whisper.

"I don't know," said Mateo, "but let's get out of here."

After a few minutes, Violet peeked over the sofa and saw the coast was clear. She took a last glance at Kokopelli and whispered, "I'm sorry. I'm going, okay?"

She felt the dancing god's gaze burning on her back as she slipped out the door.

CHAPTER 12

Violet's old truck crunched across the gravel parking lot at Maven's Haven. She came to a hasty stop, kicking up dust. She had barely slept the previous night, counting the hours to come see Hugh.

Watching him drive away angry the previous evening was a gut punch. Violet knew in that moment she had taken his presence for granted. She kept thinking about his words. *What are we doing here?* He wanted to pursue a serious relationship and she kept putting him off. After her adventures with Rosa at the Clayton ranch, the only thing she wanted to do was talk to Hugh, but with the way he left, she was afraid to call him. She resolved this morning she would tell him how she felt. Or did she even know how she felt? At any rate, she couldn't take Hugh being mad at her.

She walked toward Hugh's RV, Spirit trotting ahead. A voice shouted out behind her.

"Well, hey there!"

She swung around to see Maven standing in the office door, waving her over. Violet didn't want to be called off her mission, but Spirit was already running to say hello. She followed Maven into the office and stood at the counter.

"How's the investigation going? You found out anything yet?" said Maven, looking at Violet expectantly. Maddie came in from the back office, the same earnest expression.

So now Maven was worried?

"First of all, it's not an investigation. You're gonna get me in trouble with the sheriff, talking like that," said Violet. "I think I'm on to a few things, but I'm still putting some pieces together." Of course, she couldn't talk about anything she found at Red's place. And now that she was on the spot, Violet realized she didn't have much to report. Nothing concrete anyway.

"I can tell you this," Violet said finally. "There were a lot of people wandering around those hot springs who were not too happy with Mr. Dewer."

"It's that snake in the grass, Clayton!" Maven snapped, slapping her hand down on the counter. Maddie touched Maven's shoulder, a silent reminder to stay calm.

Violet leaned in. "Tell me this—what's the status of the development, now that Dewer's out of the picture?"

"It's at a dead standstill right now," said Maven. "It looked like Clayton was gonna try moving forward, but Dewer was the majority holder and his estate has all gone to his next of kin, his brother."

Violet tapped the counter thoughtfully as the wheels turned in her mind. "That tells us one thing. If shutting down the development was the motive, killing Dewer had the desired effect."

The three women stood in silence, pondering

for a moment.

"Well, that doesn't look good for me," said Maven. "But I'm still tickled pink the development is shut down."

"Just don't go telling that to anyone, okay?" said Violet. "Try to lay low for a few days."

Maven gave her a big wink. "You got it."

Maddie rolled her eyes. "Like that's gonna happen."

Violet made her way up the path toward Hugh's RV. Spirit knew the way and raced ahead. Hugh's cheery awning came into view. His photo-ready outdoor area reminded her of all the evenings she sat next to Hugh's fire, eating snacks and chatting. She missed those times. Maybe she shouldn't have moved out to the mesa.

Bella sat with headphones on in one of the folding chairs, her feet propped up on the fire pit. Spirit's tail wagged as Bella ruffled his fur. Hugh was nowhere to be seen. Violet gave a little wave.

Bella responded with an eye roll. She reluctantly half-removed her headphones. "My dad's not here."

"Oh. I see," said Violet. "I saw his car in the parking lot, so I thought—"

"He walked to the coffee shop," Bella interrupted.

Violet took a deep breath. She needed to find some kind of common ground with this girl.

"Spirit likes you," she ventured. "He's a good judge of character."

"I like *him* too," she said. The extra emphasis on *him* got the point across. I like him but not you.

Spirit seemed to sense the tension and came over to sit at Violet's side.

"He's going back to England, you know," said Bella. "When he's done with his book."

Violet was not good at hiding her emotions. She was certain Bella could see the blow landed, and a hint of satisfaction shone in the girl's eyes.

"He told you that?" said Violet.

Bella shrugged. "That's what he does. He stays someplace while he writes a book. And then he goes home. You didn't think he was going to spend the rest of his life in this place, did you? My mum knows she made a mistake. They're both just going through a mid-life crisis. I know him better than anyone."

Translation: *I know him better than you.*

Spirit nudged Violet's hand. "I have something —I have to do now," said Violet, backing up. "See you later, Bella."

Violet turned and walked quickly down the path. Tears stung the corners of her eyes and she blinked hard to keep them in. She just wanted to make it to her truck and get out of there.

That was going to prove difficult. Leaning up against her truck, with his arms crossed and seemingly waiting for her, was the last person she wanted to see. Oh please no, Violet thought, not now.

"If it isn't our local detective. Mrs. Deep Dish Vaughn," said Sheriff Winters. He stayed leaning against the truck, right over the driver's side door.

"I'm in a bit of a hurry," said Violet.

"Racing off to solve a crime, are ya? Gonna poke your nose where it doesn't belong?"

"I'm just trying to get my restaurant open. I need to get those deep dish pizzas cooking. Maybe you should come help me, since it looks like you don't have anything better to do."

His lip curled in distaste. "As it happens, I came to pay a visit to your buddy Maven, see if her memory's come round about what *really* happened out at the Djinn. But you were on my list of people to see today, too. Where were you last night between nine and ten? Think carefully, Deep Dish."

He knows something, Violet thought. Should she lie or try to cut him off at the pass?

"I gave my friend Rosa a ride out to the Clayton Ranch. She needed to collect some belongings."

"Is that right?" The sheriff hoisted himself off the truck to stand with his hands on his hips. He tilted his cowboy hat back so he was looking right into her eyes. "At nine o' clock at night, during a thunderstorm?"

"She wanted to go when Red wasn't home, to avoid a confrontation. She has a key. Turns out, Clayton showed up and she stayed to cook him a meal. I waited in the truck." A lot of that was actually true.

"Maybe I've gone a little too easy on you, Deep Dish." He stepped closer and then leaned down to her level. "I'm not askin' you. I'm tellin' you. Butt. Out." He punctuated the last two words with a point of his finger.

Violet stepped around him. "I have to go. I'll make sure to save some deep dish pizza for you."

She left Maven's parking lot as quickly as she could but made sure to use her blinker. She didn't want to give the sheriff any possible reason to give her a ticket—because he would. She turned onto the highway heading out of town and drove for a few minutes to make sure she was well away from Winters. Her phone dinged once and then twice. When she found a turnout, she pulled over to clear her head and check it. Maybe it was Hugh texting her, wanting her to come back to his place.

The first text was from Rosa. It read, "Police see us at Clayton's. Meet me at Deep Dish soon." A little late for that info. She was thoughtful for a moment. How did the sheriff know they were out at the Clayton Ranch?

"Of course!" she said to Spirit. "The Clayton Ranch must have cameras, probably at the entrance." Spirit cocked his head and looked interested. "If the cameras were at the house, the sheriff would have hauled me in for breaking and entering." Spirit cocked his head the other way. He was a very good listener. "But what made Clayton check the videos? Or is the sheriff staking out Clayton and just happened to see us?" Spirit lay down on the seat with a humpf and closed his eyes. Violet felt like doing the same thing.

Then she remembered the other text. It was from a number she didn't recognize. Not Hugh. She swallowed the disappointment and read, "You gave me a BOGO coupon, but I haven't given you a tour.

How's tonight look?"

Ohh. The scientist, Kent, from the observatory. She thought of Hugh again, and Bella's words. *He's going back to England, you know.* It had been such a terrible couple of days. She really did feel like doing something fun. There was nothing wrong in just going and seeing the place. "Right?" she said out loud to Spirit. His ears twitched, but he didn't look up. "Right, we're in agreement." She sent a text to Kent confirming a tour that evening.

The door to Deep Dish was locked, meaning neither Rosa nor Gabriel were there yet. Violet had planned on going home to get Rosa, but from her text, it sounded like she had arranged a ride, so Violet busied herself unloading some crates of new dishes in the kitchen. After a while, she heard the front door open and she came in the dining room to see Rosa, followed by Mateo and Bailey.

"Can you finally tell me what the big emergency is, Mom?" said Mateo, a scowl on his face. "And why did you tell me to bring Bailey with me?"

Rosa turned to Violet. "Did you get my text?"

"Yes, and thank you. But it was a little late. I ran into the sheriff first." Violet glanced at Mateo and Bailey. "I'll fill you in later."

Rosa pointed at her son. "Have a seat."

"Why?" huffed Mateo. "I've got to get to White Feather, I'm supposed to meet Dr. Wauneka at the clinic."

"Sit," ordered Rosa. "Both of you. It's truth-telling time. I asked Violet to help me keep you out of trouble Mateo. But she can't if you don't tell the truth. You too, miss."

Rosa had an authoritative manner Violet envied. The kids hopped-to and sat down.

"I was at the Clayton Ranch last night to get some of my things," said Rosa. "I heard you two talking. What's the big secret you're keeping?"

The kids looked at each other. Neither one spoke.

"Let's go," said Rosa. "Out with it."

Then the words tumbled out of Mateo's mouth, in one long rambling sentence. "Bailey saw her dad and Mr. Dewer fighting, right after I got fired, and her dad pushed Dewer and then she saw some other guy."

Bailey's eyes shot daggers at Mateo.

"I'm sorry, babe, but it's the truth," said Mateo. "It's not right to withhold this stuff. It doesn't mean your dad hurt Dewer."

"He didn't push him," said Bailey. "He just poked his finger into his chest, like this." She turned and poked Mateo. "And you were there, Mrs. Vaughn. "It was right after you and that English guy left. That was way before Mr. Dewer ended up at the Djinn."

"Mateo said you saw someone else," asked Violet. "Who was it? Why didn't you say anything about that before?"

"I don't know who he was. When my dad was arguing with Mr. Dewer, I left. I went to my Jeep thinking Mateo would be there. But he wasn't. So I went to our secret cave. There was some old guy I didn't recognize, out near the Djinn, just walking. I was afraid if I talked to the sheriff again, they'd ask me more questions about my dad, so I just—didn't say anything."

"Ay, you two!" said Rosa. "You're both just making things worse with all these secrets."

Violet nodded. "I agree. You're both gonna have to tell all this to the sheriff. But thanks for finally being honest. Bailey, can you describe the man you saw?"

"I don't know—old? He had white hair."

Violet sighed. She was so over this whole investigation thing. She just wanted to open her restaurant and enjoy the quiet desert life. After a few more questions and prodding, Rosa released the kids and they wasted no time scrambling for the door, nearly knocking Gabriel over as he entered.

"Wasn't that Mateo?" he asked, looking over his shoulder. "I would have liked to say hello."

Rosa sat down at a table. "I apologize for my son. His head is all over the place right now."

Gabriel came to sit across from her. "Is everything okay?"

Rosa covered her face with her hands. "No, everything's a mess. A week ago life was going perfectly, and now, ay Dios, everything's upside down."

Violet could see the confusion on Gabriel's face as he tried to make sense of things. She poured three mugs of coffee, sat down at the table, and proceeded to fill Gabriel in on all that was going on with Dewer's murder.

Gabriel listened wide-eyed to the story. "I don't think there's much I can do to help. But I can take care of things here at Deep Dish while you do your investigating, Mrs. Vaughn."

"Me too," Rosa put in. "I'm here for whatever you need."

The two of them looked at her with such confidence. Violet wondered what sort of aura she exuded that made all these people think she was some kind of Sherlock Holmes. She certainly didn't feel as self-assured on the inside as they seemed to see on the outside.

After a busy, and somewhat back breaking day unloading and unpacking several deliveries, Violet looked forward to the observatory visit. She checked her phone and saw a message from Kent directing her to leave her car at the base of the road to the observatory because it was a dangerous drive at night. That was fine. She looked forward to an evening of putting her troubles behind her for a while. She didn't want to face one more unexpected obstacle today.

CHAPTER 13

"I've been hearing some things about you," Kent said from behind the wheel of his black SUV. "I guess you're some kind of local celebrity."

He looked over at Violet and gave her an easy smile. Wow, he is handsome, she thought. And charming.

"Definitely not a celebrity," she said. "This— little incident—happened a few months ago and my— my friend and I got caught up in it."

"A little incident like finding your husband murdered and becoming the prime suspect, only to solve the crime yourself?"

Violet chuckled. "Yeah. That."

She was glad she agreed to let Kent drive. Although the road up to the observatory was paved, a rarity in these parts, it was steep and twisty. Kent navigated the turns expertly, having driven it many times. Even though a brilliant red and orange sunset lit up the clear sky, some areas were in near darkness as the road wound between towering cliffs.

Suddenly, Kent slammed on the brakes and Violet's seat belt dug into her chest as she pitched forward and back. A large pack of coatimundi crossed the road, single-file, their long, fat tails swaying above them.

Violet's hand remained pressed over her heart from the scare. "They're taking their sweet time, aren't they?" She let out a nervous laugh. "They are the funniest little creatures. I just love them. I'm so glad you didn't hit any."

Kent seemed lost in thought, but then realized she was speaking. "Oh yes," he said. "Me too. I love little animals and—stuff."

Violet raised an eyebrow. "That wasn't very convincing. You're not driving me to my doom, are you?"

He laughed. "No, I was spacing out, thinking about our project. We're very close to some major breakthroughs, so I'm always up in my head."

The last of the coati waddled off the road and Kent drove on.

"I'd love to hear more about the project," said Violet. "I've never been to an observatory before. Do you study the stars?"

"Planets, actually. Exoplanets, to be specific."

"I think I've heard of exoplanets," said Violet,

"But I'm painfully lacking in science knowledge. Why are they important?"

"An exoplanet is what we call planets similar to the ones in our solar system, but they orbit other stars—stars in our own galaxy, and others much farther away."

He had become quite animated as he talked about a subject close to his heart. He glanced at Violet. "How many exoplanets do you think we have in our own Milky Way galaxy?"

Violet thought for a moment. "Let's see—if each star had at least one planet, then maybe—a million?"

Kent chuckled. "Good guess, but way off. More like one hundred billion. And of those, there are possibly ten billion of the ones Fritz and I are interested in. Earth analog planets."

"Hmm. So from the name, I'm thinking those must be planets that are like Earth?"

"Correct. We look for planets that are similar to Earth and also in a habitable zone, or what we call the Goldilocks zone—an area that could sustain life."

"Oh I get it, the Goldilocks zone, because it's just right."

Kent nodded enthusiastically.

Violet felt a shiver of excitement at the prospect of so many Earth-like planets. "I always believed there must be life out there somewhere, but to actually see the numbers laid out like that, it seems like a—certainty. It's fascinating!"

Kent beamed from behind the wheel. "It's amazing work. I don't know what I'd do if I—couldn't do it anymore." His smile seemed to falter as he pondered that thought.

"Fritz is the man I met when you came into the restaurant, right? Will he be there tonight?"

"He didn't make a very good first impression, did he?" Kent shook his head. "He's a little different, but he's an excellent scientist. But no, he's down in Coatimundi tonight."

She nodded, inwardly relieved she wouldn't be seeing Fritz again. She remembered how bent out of shape he got over her misuse of a Star Trek reference.

"So, can you see these exoplanets from your telescope?" asked Violet, who was now curious to learn more about the subject.

"No, not exactly. We study the stars that the exoplanets orbit. When the star dims, we can predict that a planet passed between it and Earth. When it wobbles, that might indicate the gravitational pull of a planet."

Violet sighed. "Now we're getting to an area that sounds complicated. I'm happy to just sit here visualizing all the Earth-like planets out there and what they look like."

They came around a bend and suddenly the observatory appeared, a huge, white dome, perched on the edge of a cliff. Kent drove into a well-maintained parking lot surrounded by several small, white outbuildings. He pulled into a space with a sign that read "University Observatory. Dr. Simmons."

Violet got out and looked around. Kent's was the only car in the lot. "How many people work up here?" she asked, feeling a little nervous all of a sudden. Kent was far from threatening, but she had anticipated there would be other people at the observatory, not just the two of them.

"Normally, this place is crawling with students," said Kent, as he began to head toward the building. "But it's fall break right now. Then there's myself, Fritz and Miriam Fassie—she's a visiting astronomer from South Africa. She's spending a week in Albuquerque with her husband, so Fritz and I have been rattling around this place like mice in a tin can."

The dome rose out of a plain, square building with several single-door entrances, similar to a warehouse. Kent unlocked an unmarked door and soon Violet found herself in a long, dimly lit passage with cement floors. Doors lined the hallway on each side.

"These are the dorm rooms," said Kent, moving down the passageway. "The students and faculty stay here for long periods at times."

Violet followed, noting that some of the kids had decorated their doors with posters, pictures and stickers. Dr. Fassie's door, marked with a nameplate, had the iconic "You Are Here" poster of the galaxy with an arrow pointing at Earth. Violet wished Dr. Fassie or some of the students were here now. She could not shake an uneasy feeling, ever since arriving at the facility.

"This way," Kent called from the bottom of a spiral staircase.

Violet followed, making her way carefully up the narrow cement stairs. A security door appeared at the top of the first flight. Kent opened it and they filed into another passageway with several open doors. He led her into a room with a large window, two desks, file cabinets and various stacks of paper.

"I share this office with Fritz," said Kent. "This is where I spend a lot of my time. He tapped the keyboard of a laptop on his desk. It immediately came to life and long strips of numbers and symbols flooded the screen.

"If you don't mind hanging out here for a few, I need to go up the tower to make some adjustments. We can't see much through the big telescope until it gets a little darker anyway."

Violet glanced out the window and saw the last glow from the sunset burning out. "Sure, no problem." She sat down in his desk chair and Kent hurried out of the room.

As soon as his footsteps faded away, Violet got up and began to explore. Where Kent's desk was neat, with just the laptop, a few file folders and a water bottle, Fritz's desk was chaos.

Stacks of paper and folders fought for space with Star Trek action figures, coffee mugs and an award placard that read "Dr. Gunner Fritz". In the middle of the desk sat a large, black hard drive with a post-it on it that said "engineering". But what really caught Violet's eye was a letter partially covered by the hard drive. She could see university letterhead at the top and the word "confidential."

Of course, she shouldn't read any further. But, it was right out on the desk, albeit, mostly covered. She leaned closer to see what she could make out. "Our most recent studies indicate the---------- fundamentally changing the-------------result in the cessation of the NEXS project--------foreseeable future."

The NEXS project. Was that what Kent was working on here, or was it something different? Violet wished she could read more, but she didn't dare move the piece of equipment. She had a sudden thought of Kokopelli watching over her shoulder, shaking his feathered head and frowning.

She moved to look out the window where the canyons had turned purple and gray in the dusk. She could even see the Emerald Eyes hot spring pools glimmering far below. She glanced to her right and for the first time noticed a little alcove that held a telescope on a tripod. It was the largest telescope she had seen up close, with a barrel as big around as a coffee can. She noticed it was not pointing up at the sky, but down into the canyon. Violet couldn't resist leaning her head down to the eyepiece to take a peek.

She sucked in her breath. The image that filled the viewfinder was startlingly close. And she knew exactly what she was looking at. Even in the dim light, she could see the edge of one of the Emerald Eyes pools. It was right where she and Hugh had witnessed the incident between Dewer, Clayton, Bailey and Mateo. That was an odd thing for an astronomer to be looking at.

"Get away from that!"

Violet jumped back. She turned to see Fritz heading toward her, his face contorted in anger.

CHAPTER 14

"I'm sorry!" Violet cried, stepping away from the telescope. "I just wanted to take a quick look. I didn't touch anything."

Fritz stopped and placed his hands to his temples, then ran them back over his balding head. "That telescope is not for sightseeing. What are you doing in my office? Oh wait, don't tell me—Kent."

As if summoned, Kent came into the office and took in the scene. "What's going on? Are you alright, Violet?"

Violet came to stand next to him. "Yes, I'm fine. I, well—"

Fritz began to pace. "She was touching the *Celestron*."

Violet had worked with someone on the spectrum in the past and she recognized that Fritz might fall into the neurodivergent category. "I'm sorry, Fritz," she said sincerely. "I shouldn't have used the telescope without asking." I'm glad he didn't see me snooping on his desk, she thought.

"Yes, Fritz. She's very sorry. So drop it." Kent's voice was tight and his face tense. "I thought you had a date in town. What are you doing here?"

"She has to work early tomorrow," said Fritz. "So we made it an early night."

Violet realized that Fritz certainly looked more pulled together than the last time she saw him. He wore jeans and a blazer, with a Star Trek T-shirt underneath. A date? Well you go, Fritz, she thought. Maybe it will help with his social skills.

"I'm going to take Violet up the tower," said Kent. "And I'm gonna reposition for a few, so don't get all twitterpated, Fritz. I want to show her Saturn."

Up in the tower room, Violet waited while Kent positioned the big telescope. At first glance, the massive scope looked like a cannon ready to fire a shot through the open ceiling of the dome. It sat on a hydraulic base and there was a ladder to the side of it as well as several monitors.

Kent showed her various galactic sights, each one more amazing than the last. Finally, he positioned the scope on Saturn. She gasped when she looked through the eyepiece. The ringed planet filled the viewfinder, looking like she could reach out and touch it. The glorious bluish white rings seemed almost unreal.

Kent leaned his head near Violet's as she looked through the scope. "I wanted to show you some things you could appreciate because the stuff we normally look at wouldn't be that impressive to you."

"I'm impressed, alright. It's beautiful." She stepped away from the eyepiece, trying to put a little more distance between them. "Thank you for showing me."

Kent stepped closer. "Hey Violet, I was wondering…"

Oh no, he's going to ask me out, thought Violet. All at once she realized she didn't want him to.

"…are you seeing anyone?" he finished.

Images of Hugh came into her mind. Sitting outside his RV, joking in the car, him holding her close to take a selfie and saying *this is nice.* Suddenly, she desperately wanted to be with Hugh.

"Yes. Yes, I am." She said firmly.

"That English guy?"

Violet nodded.

"Lucky him," said Kent, his face unreadable.

"Actually, I need to be getting back," said Violet, heading for the door. "But I appreciate the tour. You don't even need to use the BOGO coupon, I'll give you a meal on the house."

"I'm looking forward to that," he said, leading the way to the door, but he sounded a little annoyed.

After a mostly-silent drive back down the mountain in the dark, Violet breathed a sigh of relief when she was finally back inside her truck and heading home. She couldn't completely wrap her head around all the weirdness at the observatory. She just knew she was glad to be out of there. And she knew something else. She was going to find Hugh right now and talk to him. Sorry, Bella, she thought. Hugh's not going back to England. Not if I can help it.

She pulled into the parking lot at Maven's Haven, noting the office was dark. That was good. She didn't want to get caught up chatting with Maven and Maddie right now. Just as she got out of the truck, she saw Hugh coming up the path. When he saw her, his pace quickened. So did hers. They ended up meeting halfway and fell into a long, tight hug.

"I was just coming to look for you," said Hugh, as they broke apart. "I've been texting you, but you didn't respond. I was getting worried."

Violet reached into her purse and pulled out her phone. "Oh my gosh, it's dead. I'm terrible with charging it. I'm sorry to worry you."

"Were you—coming to see me?" asked Hugh, reaching out to take both her hands. He looked so damned sweet and hopeful.

She squeezed his hands. "Yes. I wanted to tell you I'm sorry about the other day and—and I miss you."

"That's a coincidence. That's exactly what I texted you. I shouldn't have snapped."

Relief flooded Violet, so much so that she wobbled a little. "I have so much to tell you."

"Snacks?" he said, linking his arm through hers.

"That would be heaven."

While Hugh gathered up some food, Violet melted into a chair next to the fire pit outside. She felt her shoulders dropping. Yes, this was her happy place. Bella didn't appear to be at home, so Violet had Hugh to herself for the moment. She decided she wouldn't say anything just yet about Bella's prediction he would return to England after writing his book. The more Violet thought about it, the more she believed it was just wishful thinking on the girl's part. She hoped she might still find a way to make friends with Bella, or at least be tolerated by her anyway.

Hugh emerged from the RV with a box of crackers and packages of cheese and

salami.

"Never fear, darling, your knight has arrived." He handed her a paper plate.

"This is perfect, thank you. Hey, what's Bella up

to tonight?"

"She's over at Badlands Barbecue–with Gabriel."

"What? My Gabriel? How'd that come about?"

Hugh sat down next to Violet. "I think they met at Coati coffee. But he's a nice young man, I'm not worried about it."

It wasn't Bella Violet was worried about, but she bit her tongue.

While they noshed on their snacks and ice cold beer, Violet told Hugh about the excursion to the Clayton Ranch with Rosa and the letters she'd found. She also told him about the interview with Bailey and Mateo and the trip to the observatory.

"I get the feeling all of this fits together somehow," she said. "But I'm missing some big pieces."

"I've been thinking about that," said Hugh. "There's one avenue we haven't explored that might shed some light on the puzzle. Dewer."

Violet leaned in. "Dewer?"

"Yes. We need to know more about who he was and what he was doing the days leading up to his murder. Maybe there's someone else in his life who wanted to do him in. Judging by how sour he appeared, it seems likely."

"I hadn't even thought of that. Maven says

his brother inherited everything, so he must not be married."

"I did a little poking around. I guess Dewer was somewhat of a loner. He lives—um, lived, in a mansion in the desert near Albuquerque. You want to take a little field trip in the morning?"

Violet was thoughtful. "Well—I promised Kokopelli I wouldn't snoop anymore. I feel like I'm pushing my luck lately."

Hugh added a log to the fire. "Maybe that Kokopelli needs to mind his own business. And I ask you—is it really snooping if the person is—no longer with us?"

It didn't take much to twist Violet's arm. "I like your thinking. What time should we head out?"

CHAPTER 15

The blue Mini zipped along the highway toward Albuquerque, Hugh at the wheel. The clear bright morning set the desert landscape alight in brilliant orange, rust and green. The ever changing colors and panoramas of New Mexico continued to thrill Violet. She rolled down the window a bit and inhaled the smell of sage and earth. She was also feeling another thrill–being back in her sweet spot, next to Hugh. She took a sip of her Mexican cocoa cappuccino from Coati Coffee. Yes, life was sweet.

Hugh interrupted her reverie. "Montoya hasn't been able to get any information on the bandit biker who attacked us."

So much for serenity, she thought. Back to reality. "What about the pictures I took?"

"Unfortunately, there wasn't anything identifying in the pictures. And they haven't been able to trace the IP address he sent the email from. It's a fake account."

"How about the work on your book? Have you been able to make any connections about the White

Feather killer from everything you've learned so far?"

Hugh put on a mock serious face. "I guess you'll have to wait for my book to come out."

Violet swatted his arm. "Seriously."

"Okay, seriously. I'm making some connections, but I'm still working some things out. But this is just between you and me. I've had several confirmations of a white pickup truck with a Caucasian driver seen talking to some of the victims before they disappeared. I believe the man who attacked us might be the same guy. He's physically fit. He's got some money. He's local, maybe from Coatimundi. He's close enough that he knows I'm researching the case. And he's familiar to the victims, maybe a shopkeeper or bartender–not a total stranger to them, so they let their guard down."

Violet thought about all the men she interacted with on a daily basis in Coatimundi. Could one of them be a serial killer? What a dreadful thought.

"Montoya's doing some really good work on the case," said Hugh. "She's working closely with the tribal police and giving them some resources they didn't have access to before. Like processing DNA and other forensic evidence."

"They have DNA evidence?"

"Montoya won't tell me what they've got, but I suspect they do."

Violet looked out at the desert vista and felt a pang in her heart for Rainey Wauneka and her heartbroken siblings. She prayed justice would come soon. Her thoughts wandered to Dewer's murder.

"As for today's mission, any idea what we might find?" She asked Hugh. "I'm sure the authorities have already been to his house."

"I'm not sure about that," said Hugh. "Sheriff Winters seems honed-in on Maven."

"And I think Mateo is his back-up suspect."

Hugh nodded. "Mateo certainly isn't out of the woods either. I did hear a little rumor that they might bring Montoya onto the case. She's nearby, and the FBI has more resources than the county sheriff."

"Does she have jurisdiction?"

"Apparently Dewer was already under investigation for corruption and financial crimes involving another building project."

Violet's eyes went wide. "You're just now telling me this? That's big!"

"We've had a lot of ground to cover."

Violet sighed. "That we have."

Sporadic housing developments and businesses signaled they were approaching Albuquerque. Hugh followed the GPS directions and they began winding through an upscale development. As they drove up into the hills, the property sizes became bigger and bigger, with fabulous homes dotting the landscape. Each mansion followed the same theme, with sand-colored adobe and desert landscaping. But the architecture and designs were all different. Violet and Hugh oohed and aahed as one breathtaking home seemed to top the previous one.

Finally, Hugh pulled up in front of the entry gates for Dewer's place. The gates were open, but he parked out on the road.

Violet peered toward the house. "What's the plan?"

"I don't really know. I thought we'd figure it out when we got here. Sometimes things just seem to fall into place if you don't over think it."

Violet gave a nervous laugh. "And sometimes when you don't plan, you get attacked by a masked biker."

"Touché," he said. "Come on. Let's see what we find."

They peered around one of the columns supporting the entry gates and saw a long, curving drive bordered by rock gardens. Purple sage and prickly pear cactus dotted the scenery. The single-level mansion looked more like a small village than a home, with porticos branching out here and there, and breezeways running between sections of the house.

Violet nudged Hugh and pointed up the drive. Two cars were parked in front of an arched entrance area.

Hugh nodded and gestured toward one of several large, green bushes that decorated the rock garden.

"Let's hide over there and get the lay of the land," he whispered. He took her hand and they ran to the shrubbery, arranging themselves where they were hidden but could still see the front of the house. They had barely made it to the spot when two people emerged from the entryway, a man and a woman. Both were well-dressed, he in a suit and she in a green dress. They approached one of the vehicles and the man opened the trunk. After rummaging around, he pulled out a square piece of metal and a hammer. He made his way into some of the bordering gravel and began installing a sign.

"Realtors!" Hugh whispered.

Violet nodded, keeping her eyes on the pair. The sign in place, the realtors got into their car and headed down the drive, leaving one car still there. Hugh and Violet withdrew deeper into the shrubbery until the car passed through the gates.

"What should we do now?" whispered Violet.

Hugh appeared to be thinking, but suddenly, someone else emerged from the home, a middle-aged woman carrying a caddy filled with cleaning supplies and a mop. Violet and Hugh exchanged looks. The woman put her supplies in the trunk and went back in the house.

"I have an idea," said Violet, "but we have to hurry. We need our car." She took his hand, and they ran back to the driveway and through the entrance. She quickly told Hugh her plan and they drove the Mini through the gate and up the drive. Violet made sure to note the name of the realty company on the yard sign. Thankfully, she had dressed presentably today in a pink mohair sweater, jeans and boots. Hugh wore his signature sweater vest. They saw a different cleaning woman emerge from the house, carrying a vacuum cleaner.

"Let's go," said Violet.

They exited the Mini and walked past the woman with the vacuum. The other woman was leaving the house again, carrying another bucket. She looked like she was going to speak, but Violet stopped her.

"Vista Realty," said Violet, and then continued toward the front door.

"Wasn't you guys just here?" asked the woman, sounding annoyed.

Hugh followed Violet. "That was the setup team. We're the super seller startup team. Hey, you looking to buy or sell?"

The woman continued toward the car. "Do I look like I can afford this place?"

"I have properties in every range," Hugh called after her.

She put her bucket in the trunk and then headed back toward them.

"We're supposed to lock up," she said. "So you'd better put the lock box on when you leave or it's gonna be my butt."

"Have you been cleaning for the owner for very long?" asked Violet.

"Nope, this is our first time. And it'll be our last. It's nothing but a creepy graveyard in there. Oh, and someone needs to do something about that bird. That's just not right."

With that, she went back to her car and the two women got in and drove away, leaving Violet and Hugh to ponder her cryptic words.

"That was weird," said Violet. "I'm afraid to see what's in there. But we'd better hurry before someone else comes along."

"Agreed. Your plan worked well though. See, sometimes under-thinking pays off."

"I wonder what she meant about the bird?" said Violet, making her way toward the front door. The cleaning ladies had left it ajar and she could smell the

scent of Pine Sol coming from within, mixed with–
what was it?

"Can you smell that?" she asked Hugh.

"It's rather–musty, isn't it?"

"Yes, that's the right word."

Hugh pushed the tall, solid wooden door. It swung open slowly and silently.

"Nothing ventured, nothing gained," joked Hugh, as he stepped over the threshold. Then he jumped back, almost knocking Violet over.

"Bloody hell!"

CHAPTER 16

"What is it?" cried Violet.

"It's–oh, that gave me a fright. It's okay, come on in."

Violet entered cautiously, her heart pounding. She soon saw the source of the scare. Just a few feet inside stood a very large, very real grizzly bear, standing on its hind legs, in full growl. Very dead, though.

"It's taxidermy," said Hugh, moving closer to the bear.

Violet looked past the bear to take in more of the entry hall. Animals crouched, perched and lazed everywhere, frozen in time.

"Ugh. Dewer must have been a trophy hunter," said Violet, disgust thick in her voice. "Imagine these poor creatures' last vision was of him."

Hugh looked around the room. "I think we also know the source of the musty smell. The poor little buggers are everywhere."

They began to make their way through the large front hall.

"Let's see if we can find the office," said Violet.

They passed a large open kitchen and living room. Besides the taxidermy, the home had an animal print theme, with zebra-striped pillows and leopard print throws.

Hugh pulled a blanket off the arm of the sofa and draped it over his shoulder. "Me Tarzan, you Jane." He beat his chest with both fists.

Violet choked down her laughter. "Come on, Tarzan, I want to get out of here." She peered into a room further up the hall. "Aha! Office."

The two made their way into a large room dominated by a massive oak desk. The office also contained more of the stuffed animals and walls filled with framed photos. Violet went to peer closer at one and realized they were mostly trophy photos of Dewer and his kills. She shivered and stepped away.

"Look over here," said Hugh. He stood in front of two easels, each holding a large, colorful cardboard display. "It's his plans for the Emerald Eyes resort. But this isn't just a housing development. It's a hotel casino."

Violet came to inspect the displays. Indeed, the plans appeared to be for a vast casino property. In the rendering, the Emerald Eyes hot springs pools were surrounded with cement patio areas, complete with lounge chairs and umbrellas.

"Now I see what Clayton was arguing with him about," said Violet, peering closely at the displays. "If the citizens of Coatimundi caught wind of these plans, it would certainly ruin his chances of becoming mayor."

Hugh nodded. "And didn't you tell me his wife was going to cut him off if he continued with his big schemes?"

Violet's thoughts were interrupted by a rustling sound. She spun around. "Did you hear that?"

Hugh was already walking toward a corner of the room. It was the first time Violet noticed a bird cage.

"Oh dear," said Hugh, from across the room.

Violet hurried to his side. Her jaw dropped at what she saw. At the bottom of a filthy cage, amidst mounds of soiled and torn newspapers, sat the saddest looking bird she had ever seen. He looked something like a gray parrot, but he was missing large patches of feathers, right down to his delicate pink skin.

"Poor little chap," Hugh said gently. "I had an African Gray growing up. They're brilliant birds. This cage is far too small for him. The patchy feathers are a sign of neglect. He is so stressed out, he's pulling out his feathers."

"What should we do?"

"Only thing we can do," said Hugh. "He's coming with us."

Violet nodded in agreement.

Hugh murmured gently to the bird and began removing the water container to fill it. Violet continued looking around the office.

"Dewer was mega-rich," Hugh called over to her as he worked on the bird cage. "You say the brother inherited the whole enchilada?"

"Yes, according to Maven." Violet leaned in to view a photo on the wall, one of the few not showing Dewer with a fresh kill.

"The money alone is a huge motive," said Hugh. "But how do we find the brother?"

"I think I just did," said Violet. She pointed at the photo.

Hugh came over to stand next to her and they examined the recent photograph. Dewer stood next to a man who looked exactly like him in features. But the similarity stopped there. The twin brother wore a cheerful smile, a twinkle in his eye, and—the robes of a monk.

"His brother—is a brother," said Hugh.

"Look at the sign behind them," Violet whispered.

"Monastery of Benedict in the Desert," read Hugh.

"I've heard of that place," said Violet. "They sold produce at the harvest festival."

"I say we pay the good brother a visit. On the pretense of bringing him the bird," said Hugh.

"Yes, we'd better get a move-on."

But they froze in their tracks at the sound of clicking footsteps on the tile hallway.

"Who's in here?" a voice called out.

CHAPTER 17

The woman's voice sounded close. Violet looked around wildly and saw zero places to hide. She grabbed Hugh's arm. "Quick! Get the bird!"

Hugh sprung into action and picked up the birdcage, just as a woman walked through the office door. It was the green dress realtor. Her surprised eyes moved back and forth between Violet and Hugh.

Violet did her best to emit a confident air. She pointed at the cage. "Humane Society. We're here for the bird."

The realtor's shoulders dropped as relief swept her face. "Oh, thank goodness. That's one less thing on my plate. This place is gonna be hard enough to show, as it is."

Hugh moved toward the door. "We'll just be on our way then."

The realtor seemed to melt at Hugh's voice. "Well, hello mister British accent. I'm an animal lover, too. You live here in Albuquerque?"

Hugh seemed to be taken off guard by the flirting and could only mumble, "Uhh..."

"We need to get this bird to a vet," said Violet. She pulled Hugh's sleeve and headed for the door.

"Give me a call if you're looking for a property–or something," the realtor called after them.

"I'm pretty sure she doesn't mean me," Violet joked, as they hot-footed it down the hall. On his way through the living room, Hugh grabbed one of the animal print throws and used it to cover the bird cage.

"You sure you don't want to get her card?" Violet teased when they were out of earshot of the woman. "She is an animal lover, after all."

"Tarzan already have Jane. And–Edward." He held the birdcage aloft.

"Edward? That's–an interesting name for a bird."

"It's a proper British name. The little chap needs some dignity."

"Don't get too attached." Violet warned. "The plan is to bring him to Dewer's brother."

"If Brother Dewer wanted the bird, I expect he would have already come to get him."

Violet glanced at Hugh and recognized his resolute expression. He's not giving up this bird, she thought. Somehow that knowledge made her heart flutter.

"We've managed to get past several people, just by pretending we belong," Hugh said cheerily as they loaded Edward in the car.

Violet put on an angelic face. "Maybe we just look innocent."

Hugh waggled his eyebrows. "Little do they know."

Back on the road, some quick googling got them directions to the monastery, which was in the desert near White Feather.

Hugh put the coordinates into the GPS. "That's good, we can bring Edward to Dr. Wauneka's clinic after the monastery." He glanced at Violet. "If the brother doesn't want to keep him, that is."

Violet listened distractedly as the events of the morning swirled around her head. She noticed Hugh glancing over at her.

"Uh-oh, I know that look," he said. His eyes scanned the landscape on both sides of the road. "Food?"

All Violet could do was nod. Hugh was beginning to know her better than she knew herself. She was starving. And the outskirts of Albuquerque didn't appear to offer many choices.

"How about this place?" Hugh slowed the car and pulled into the dusty lot of an unassuming pale pink adobe building with a sign that read: "Salvadoran Food. Pupusas!"
He peeked through the blanket at Edward. "We can't leave him in here too long. Maybe we can get something quick."

Violet nodded in agreement. "I'll take anything right now."

They opened the door to a packed restaurant. Wait staff bustled around with trays full of steaming and delicious-smelling food. A waitress pointed them to a table.

"We don't have much time," Hugh told her. "Is there something quick we can eat?"

She nodded and pointed again for them to sit down. Within minutes, the same waitress appeared and placed large bowls of steaming soup in front of them. In the center of the table she set a plate loaded with hot, puffy tortillas, the blackened marks on their surface looking like a moonscape.

"Have you had Salvadoran food before?" the waitress asked.

They shook their heads.

She pointed at the soup. "Caldo de res. And Salvadoran tortillas."

Violet thanked her and turned to her meal. The soup consisted of a fragrant broth with large, tender chunks of beef as well as potatoes, carrots, zucchini, cabbage and two-inch sections of corn on the cob.

After a few minutes of savoring the meal, Violet put her spoon down. "This might be the most perfect soup I've ever tasted."

"Indeed. It's delicious. Wait, don't tell me, you're going to steal it for Deep Dish."

"I'm sure it's a traditional soup, so it's not really stealing. But yes. I was thinking I could replace the zucchini with some of the interesting squash from the harvest festival. I'm pretty sure it was the monks who were selling squash there."

"From Brother Dewer's monastery?"

"I'm assuming so. "There can't be that many monasteries around here."

Back in the car, they checked on Edward, who peered at them silently from the bottom of his cage with big, frightened eyes. Violet looked forward to getting the little guy to Dr. Wauneka's clinic for some TLC. Unless Dewer's brother wanted to keep him, that is. While they drove, she called Gabriel to check in on the happenings at Deep Dish.

"We just got the shipment of flour put away and Rosa's learning how to use the stove," he said jovially. Violet wondered how she got so lucky to find such an enthusiastic manager.

"And don't forget, Mrs. Vaughn, I have to leave early today, but Rosa's gonna stay here with Spirit until you get back. And–hang on–Rosa wants to know if you found out anything."

"No major breakthroughs." Violet felt terrible that Rosa was suffering with worry over her son. "But tell her–tell her not to worry, we're going to find out all we can."

They traveled a winding road through the desert which eventually paralleled a river. The landscape became more lush as swathes of greenery bordered the sparkling blue water that cut through the valley. The monastery appeared at the base of craggy, red mountains. They approached the sand-colored priory and found themselves surrounded by fields of squash and pumpkins. The vines, now shriveled this late in the season, contained only the occasional fruit.

"Wow," Hugh murmured. "Almost makes me

want to become a monk."

"It is beautiful," Violet agreed. "But you'd have to give up women, Tarzan."

"Scratch that. Maybe I'll just visit."

"That might be an option." She pointed to a sign that read "Guest House."

They found a place to park and began to walk up a perfectly-maintained, pebbled path toward the main building.

Violet looked at Hugh and chuckled. "That birdcage is becoming your new accessory."

Hugh adopted a high-brow accent. "Dahling, animal prints are quite the thing this season."

"The poor little guy must wonder what in the world is happening," she said seriously. "Hopefully we can sort out his future and get some answers from Dewer's brother at the same time."

The monastery itself consisted of a domed building in the center with adjacent wings branching out on three sides. Each of the wings had covered walkways that ran their length. Vines crawled and tumbled around the supporting pillars. A spire rose from the building toward the sky with a little alcove on top encasing a small bell. At that moment, the bell started to ring. Monks wearing black robes began to emerge from the building, alone or in pairs.

A young, dark-haired monk headed slowly down the path toward them and stopped as they drew near.

"May I help you find something?" he asked, his voice pleasant and kind. He glanced at the birdcage.

"May I?"

Hugh nodded and the monk peeked through the blanket. He looked back at them with understanding. "I'm sorry, but the blessing of the animals was two weeks ago. And it looks like your little friend needed it."

"Actually, we're looking for, uh–Brother Dewer," said Hugh.

The young man stared back blankly. "Brother Dewer?" Then a smile of realization crossed his face. "Oh, you must mean Prior Kenneth."

"Yes, of course," said Violet, "Prior Kenneth."

"Is the prior your head man?" Hugh asked.

"He's our spiritual leader, but I guess you could say that." He glanced again at the birdcage, a little uncertain now. "Follow me."

He turned and headed back up the path toward the main building. Violet breathed in the peaceful, fragrant air of the monastery and felt her shoulders drop. She wouldn't mind coming to spend more time here under different circumstances. They passed through an archway and into a courtyard filled with greenery, statues and benches. Finally, he led them into a side door and they arrived in an airy office with terra cotta tile floors and simple wooden furniture.

Violet recognized Prior Kenneth right away. He sat at a table filled with neat stacks of paperwork. He wore the same black robes as all the other monks, looking exactly like–and nothing like his brother. He smiled at the young monk and at Violet and Hugh.

"What's this you've brought me, Brother

Andrew? Come in, come in." Prior Kenneth looked at them expectantly.

Violet spoke up. "First, we want to offer our sincere condolences on the death of your brother."

He drew his hands together in prayer and dipped his head. "That's kind of you, thank you. Is–is that why you're here?" His eyes flicked to the bird cage and then back at them.

"We've brought his bird," said Violet, gesturing at the cage.

"Oh–my," the prior stuttered. "I didn't realize Gavin still had that bird." He looked thoughtful for a moment then remembered his hosting duties. "Do you need chairs? Some tea? We'll have some tea, yes, that sounds good."

A monk in the back of the room nodded and left the room, presumably to get refreshments. Another monk pulled two rustic wooden chairs close to the prior's desk and Violet and Hugh sat.

Violet realized this was the first time learning the dead man's name was Gavin. She had only thought of him as Dewer up until this moment.

"Of course, if you don't want the bird, I'm happy to keep him," Hugh offered.

Prior Kenneth scanned Hugh's face, then nodded. "It seems the creature has found a new home– and a good deal better one than where he came from. But that's not the only reason you're here, is it?"

"No," said Violet. "We want to ask you some questions about your brother. We're looking into his death. You were the sole heir to his fortune–"

"You think I'm a suspect?"

"Oh, well, no…" Violet stammered.

"Not necessarily," Hugh put in.

"Brother Mathias!" the prior yelled.

Within seconds, a large, bald and burly monk came into the room. "What is it?"

"I'm a suspect!" the prior cried.

Violet stood up. "We didn't mean to upset you, I'm so sorry!"

Prior Kenneth stood up as well. "You don't understand. This is–this is wonderful!"

CHAPTER 18

Violet and Hugh stared at Prior Kenneth in confusion. Violet wondered if perhaps the monk had taken leave of his senses.

The prior's smile widened. "I suppose that must sound strange to you. Please, Mrs. Vaughn have a seat and I'll explain."

Violet sat. She glanced at Hugh. By the puzzled look on his face, she knew he was as bewildered as she was.

A young monk entered the room carrying a tray with a teapot and mugs. While Prior Kenneth served them all, Violet was dying to know how anyone could think being a suspect was wonderful. Having recently been a suspect herself, she remembered the experience as decidedly awful. But it appeared everything at the monastery moved at a measured pace, so she waited. The prior handed her an earthenware mug. The handle-less vessel appeared ancient. Hand-forged and glazed a bluish gray tint, the hot mug comforted her. She inhaled the spicy, strong black tea and watched the prior adjust his robes to settle back into his chair.

"I apologize for my outburst," he said finally. "I allowed my excitement to overtake me for a moment. We try to avoid outbursts here, but alas, we are human." He smiled at the burly Brother Mathias, who nodded and smiled back.

"You see," he continued. "Myself, Brother Mathias, and a few others here are mystery fans. We have a group that meets weekly and we're writing our own mystery novel that takes place at a monastery. I never thought one of us would ever have anything so exciting happen as being a suspect. Everything here is the same, day in and day out–that's what we strive for, of course."

"Perhaps we can write this into the book," Brother Mathias suggested.

"Yes! Good thinking! Brother, will you take notes on the questions our friends here have come to ask–after I stop babbling, that is?"

Hugh leaned forward. "Prior Kenneth–excuse me, I don't know much about monastic life, but I'm surprised at your interest in mysteries–or that you're allowed to explore that type of dark material."

The prior nodded. "Yes, I see how one might think that. But we're a Benedictine sect. We follow the teachings of St. Benedict. Our belief is, that which is not sinful may be enjoyed in moderation. Mysteries are part of the human condition. They also highlight the struggle between good and evil."

Violet nodded thoughtfully. "I guess good and evil are your territory."

The prior's hand touched the simple, wood-carved crucifix strung on leather around his neck. "Hopefully more good than evil."

"As we mentioned before, we'd like to ask some questions about your brother," said Violet. "What can you tell us about the development he was planning at the Emerald Eyes Hot Springs?"

"Oh, that goes way back," said the prior thoughtfully. He steepled his fingers in front of him. "Gavin bought that land a long time ago. We used to go out to the hot springs when we were kids. He always told me he was going to give it to the monastery. But over the years, Gavin…changed. Then he met that Red Clayton fellow. He owns some of the adjoining property. He's from Coatimundi, perhaps you know him?"

Violet and Hugh exchanged looks. "Oh yes," said Hugh, "We know him."

The prior's quick eyes noticed. "Yes, he's a schemer. He and my brother were two peas in a pod. At any rate, Gavin went back on his word. He decided to develop the Emerald Eyes area instead of giving it to the monastery. Of the seven deadly sins, he practiced most of them. But greed was the deadliest."

He turned to Brother Mathias. "Did you get that part about greed?"

"Oh yes," said the brother, writing furiously. "This is good stuff."

Violet leaned in. "If you'll forgive me, that sounds like a strong motive."

"It is, isn't it!"

"You're not uncomfortable with people thinking you might be a murderer?"

"I think I might be uncomfortable if I didn't have a–what do they call it? A rock solid alibi? The day Gavin died, I was here, at the monastery. Dozens of people can vouch for me."

"You should put that in too," Hugh said to Brother Mathias. "About the alibi. But don't say 'rock solid.' That's a little cliché. Maybe–"

"Preordained?" suggested Violet.

Prior Kenneth clapped his hands together. "Much better!"

Violet found herself liking Prior Kenneth immensely. "One last question," she said. "Do you know of anyone who might have wanted to harm your brother?"

The prior's face turned sad. "I'm afraid that might be a long list. But truth be told, we've rarely seen each other over the years."

Prior Kenneth's gaze looked to the door and Violet turned to see a young monk standing in the entryway. He clutched a sheet of paper in his hands and appeared agitated, shifting from one foot to the other.

The prior waved him in. "Brother Quan, you look like you have toads in your robes, we've talked about this–"

"But prior..." The young man quickly approached the desk.

The prior moved his hands slowly through the air, as if conducting. "Measured pace, brother. Pray. Breathe. Then speak. Now, what is it?"

Brother Quan thrust the sheet of paper toward Prior Kenneth. "We found this in the chapel, addressed to you."

Violet watched as the prior scanned the letter. His eyes widened in astonishment.

"Well, well, well," he said, shaking his head. "The proverbial plot thickens."

He laid the letter on the table and turned it so Violet and Hugh could see. Brothers Mathias and Quan crowded around the desk.

The white sheet of paper contained just a few words, scrawled in black Sharpie.

STOP EMERALD EYES DEVELOPMENT OR ELSE!

"An actual threatening letter!" Prior Kenneth cried gleefully. "We must call an emergency meeting of the mystery group!" He then seemed to realize his emotional outburst and collected himself, donning a serene expression. "After vespers, of course."

Violet scanned the letter again. Something about it seemed to niggle at the back of her mind.

"One thing's certain," Hugh said. "This writer also needs to work on their creative skills.'Or else' is another cliché."

The prior nodded. "Or die would be better."

"I think you all need to concentrate on the seriousness of this," said Violet. "Aren't you worried for your safety?"

"No," said the prior. "First of all, my safety is God's will."

He clasped his hands in prayer, and bowed his head. Brothers Mathias and Quan dutifully followed.

The prior looked up and continued. "Second of all, I'd already planned to stop the development. I'll give the land to the church, of course. I've always hoped to make it a protected sanctuary. But no one else knows that yet."

He picked the letter up off the table. "Obviously, the writer of our little note doesn't know. You know who should be worried? Gavin's partner in the project, that Clayton fellow. If the killer is trying to stop the development, he may be at risk."

"Unless he's the killer," said Violet.

"That wouldn't make sense," said the prior. "Why would he want to stop the development?"

"Because the project was spiraling out of control," said Hugh. "Clayton agreed to a small housing development. But Dewer expanded the scope to a hotel casino, which would wipe out the hot springs for all intents and purposes."

"Clayton's running for mayor," Violet put in. "If the residents of Coatimundi get wind of the scope of the project, he's sure to lose. Plus, his wife is against the project and she's threatening to cut him off financially."

Prior Kenneth listened intently. Brother Mathias scribbled notes.

"Now–how did you two say you knew my brother?" the prior asked.

Violet set her mug down. "We didn't. But the sheriff's eyeing our friend Maven as the chief suspect. She also wanted to stop the development. But she would never hurt anyone–I'm certain of it. Maven's a peace lover."

"As am I," said the prior. "I wish you well on your investigation. I have to prepare for vespers now–that's our afternoon prayers. You're welcome to join us in the chapel."

"We'd best be on our way," said Hugh. "But you should contact the authorities about that letter. And–good luck with your novel."

CHAPTER 19

Violet and Hugh made their way back through the garden courtyard. They emerged through the gate and spied Brother Quan walking on a side path toward the chapel. This time, he appeared to be consciously moving at a painfully slow pace, no doubt practicing after the admonishment from Prior Kenneth.

"We should ask him more about the letter," said Violet. We need to know what time it was placed in the chapel or if anyone saw anything. Excuse me!" she called. "Brother Quan, could we have a word?"

He smiled and paused, waiting for them to catch up.

"Sorry to bother," said Hugh. "We were wondering about the letter you found. Do you know when it might have been placed there?"

The monk put his hand on his chin and thought for a moment. "It came in through the mail hatch in the side door to the chapel, where we get all our mail. But it was hand-delivered–there was no postage. It could have come any time since we checked the mail yesterday."

"Did anyone see a stranger in the area?" asked Violet.

"We've asked around, but no one's seen any visitors today—other than you folks. Do you think…do you think Prior Kenneth's in danger?"

"Not necessarily," said Hugh, "But someone is intent on stopping the development at Emerald Eyes. You might want to tighten security around here for a while."

The monk nodded. "Understood. I'll let the brothers know."

Brother Quan looked past Violet and Hugh toward the parking area. "Oh look, here's another visitor."

Violet swung around to see a small woman in a sharp suit striding intently up the path, her eyes shooting daggers at them. Agent Montoya.

"Uh-oh," Hugh whispered. "She's not gonna be happy with us."

Brother Quan waved her over. "Greetings. The prayer service is about to get started." He pointed toward the chapel. "Right through there."

The agent glared at Violet and Hugh, then spoke to the monk. "I'm here to see Prior Kenneth Dewer. I expect these two are here for the same thing."

Violet wanted to make some kind of excuse but felt wrong lying while standing in front of the chapel on the monastery grounds. She was already in trouble with Kokopelli. She didn't want to send even more sins to Upper Management.

"They've just spoken to him," said the monk. "And he's getting ready for the service. If you join us, you can speak with him after. I need to be going myself." He bowed his head then hurried away, remembered himself and slowed his pace.

Montoya turned her full attention to Violet and Hugh. She put her hands on her hips and tilted her head. "So?" She waited a moment, tapping her foot. "You might as well just tell me."

"Prior Kenneth was promised the Emerald Eyes property for the Church," said Hugh. "But Dewer went back on his word."

"He's being threatened as well, maybe by the killer," Violet put in. "He got a letter while we were here, telling him to stop the development."

"Silly me," said Montoya dryly. "Here I thought you were gonna apologize for continuing to butt into an active investigation. Something you've been continually warned about. Is there any way I can make it clearer, or do I need to charge you two with obstruction and have you wait out this investigation in the Coatimundi jail? Maybe you enjoyed your stay there, Mrs. Vaughn, and you're anxious to go spend more time with Sheriff Winters?"

The mention of the surly sheriff sent shivers up Violet's spine. "I'm just looking out for my friend," she said. "I don't want to see Maven get pigeon-holed by the sheriff, like I did. She's innocent."

"Leave the sheriff to me," said Montoya. "Just... go work on your restaurant, or write your book or walk your dog." Her eyes drifted down to the birdcage, which Hugh had set on the ground. "What's with the, um...what is that?"

Hugh lifted the cage. "It's Dewer's bird. He

neglected it. We came here to give it to his brother, Prior Kenneth. But he doesn't want him. The bird, I mean, not the brother. His name's Edward."

"Do I need to ask how you obtained this bird?"

Hugh cleared his throat. "No, you'd better not."

Montoya lifted the blanket and peered inside. The parrot looked frightened and forlorn at the bottom of the cage. Violet knew animals were Montoya's Achilles heel.

The agent visibly melted, her face softening. "Oh...poor little thing. What's happened to him?"

"African Grays are very smart and sensitive birds," said Hugh. "When they're neglected or stressed, they pull out their feathers. When treated properly, they can live sixty, seventy years, or beyond. The one I had growing up is still living with my mum in Nottingham. I'll get Edward healthy again. In fact, we were heading to see Kai Wauneka right now."

At the mention of the handsome vet's name, Violet thought she detected a little coloring of Montoya's cheeks.

"Well...alright then," she said. "Get to it. And–"

"We know," said Violet. "Stay out of the investigation."

Back on the road, Violet watched the afternoon sun glint off the river. Her thoughts drifted to the jolly prior and the peaceful environs of the monastery.

"Do you think Prior Kenneth could have killed his brother?" she asked Hugh. "He seems so nice."

Hugh shrugged. "Nice people can also be killers. But I hope not. Just like I hope it wasn't Maven."

"You hope? You mean, you think it's possible Maven did it?"

"Anything's possible. But I think we're dealing with something bigger than we imagined. There's pieces to the puzzle I can't figure out yet."

Violet sank into her seat. "I get the same feeling. Just like with the last murder we dealt with, there's something at the back of my mind that I just can't put together—"

She was interrupted by her cell phone ringing. Rosa. She hit speaker and hadn't even said hello when Rosa's agitated voice called out.

"Violet! You have to get back here...quickly!"

Violet's throat went dry. "Why, what is it? Is Spirit okay?"

"It's Mr. Clayton. He's been shot!"

CHAPTER 20

Hugh put his foot on the gas and they began to speed toward home.

"Rosa, are you still there?" Violet held her hand to her chest. "What happened? Are you okay?"

"Yes, yes, I'm okay. I just want to get to the hospital, but I have Spirit with me."

"Take him over to my place," Hugh said, "Bella's there, she'll watch him."

"Okay, I will," said Rosa, her voice shaking.

"Do you know what happened?" asked Violet.

"Dr. Wauneka and Mateo went out to take care of a sick lamb. When they got there, they found Mr. Clayton lying in the road, bleeding. He'd been shot and who knows how long he'd been there like that. Oh, I really have to go, I have to get to the hospital."

"Wait," said Violet. "I thought you were angry with Red, why–"

"I am angry with him," Rosa interrupted, tears filling her voice. "But he's family."

"I understand. Thanks for letting me know," said Violet, "We'll meet you over there."

By the time they pulled up to the little hospital in Coatimundi, the sky was beginning to color with another brilliant New Mexico sunset. Sheriff Winters stood outside, talking to his girlfriend Jennifer. Her vibrant red hair shone almost as brightly as the sky and she clutched a little Chihuahua in her arms.

The couple were so involved in their conversation they didn't notice Violet and Hugh walking toward them. Hugh still carried the bird cage for lack of any other option. Violet put a hand on Hugh's sleeve to stop him so she could make out the conversation.

"I don't know why you won't let me go, Dan, that's my brother in there."

"Half brother," he said. "And you haven't exactly been welcomed into the family with open arms."

"Well maybe it's time that changed."

"Look–Jen Jen. Pookums," the sheriff purred, causing bile to rise in Violet's throat. "I'm running an investigation and it's already becoming a zoo in there."

"So you're saying I'm a zoo animal, is that it?" Jennifer huffed.

"I'm saying go home. I'll call you when I know more." The sheriff strode towards the hospital, luckily not turning around. But they couldn't escape Jennifer who spun on her heel and started at the sight of them standing there.

"What are you two looking at?" she barked in her characteristic bossy tone. "Were you spying on us?"

"Hello, lovely to see you," said Hugh, taking

Violet's arm. "Gotta run, cheerio." They hurried past her and through the door to the hospital, leaving Jennifer with her mouth agape. Violet marveled once again at how handy Hugh was to have around.

Sheriff Winters was right. Zoo was a good description of the packed waiting room. The Coatimundi hospital was far removed from the modern clinics of present day. The place felt more like a ski lodge than a health center, with overstuffed Navajo-print loveseats scattered around, Southwestern art on the wall and even a brick fireplace where a small pile of logs crackled invitingly.

Townsfolk gathered in small groups–in the chairs, by the fire or scattered around the room, as if they were at a cocktail party and not a hospital. The shooting of Red Clayton was looking to be *the* event of the season.

Violet scanned the crowd. Mateo and Bailey sat huddled together on one of the love seats. Sheriff Winters and Deputy Brody Clayton stood in the hallway talking to Kai Wauneka. Maven huddled in a corner with Maddie and some other locals. She saw Violet and Hugh and waved them over.

Violet gave Maven's shoulder a squeeze. "How's Red doing? Is he going to make it?"

"Shot in the arm," Maddie put in. "He'll be fine, he's already stitched up."

Violet nodded. "I'm surprised to see you here, Maven. You and Red aren't exactly best buddies."

Maven let out a hoot and slapped her leg, jangling

her armload of turquoise bracelets. "You got that right. A lot of people don't see eye to eye with Red Clayton. But he's one of us. He's a Coatimundian, and we protect our own."

Violet nodded and tried to wrap her head around the mentality of these locals. Coming from a big city like Chicago, it wasn't something she was used to. She remembered her conversation with Rosa earlier. *Yes, I'm angry with him. But he's family.*

Maven warmed to her subject and had now attracted a crowd, with lots of nodding and cheering her on. "I tell you what, that killer went a step too far when he shot one of us."

Another round of cheers.

"I agree," came a voice, pushing through the crowd. Sheriff Winters. "Someone went a step too far. Someone who was angry with Dewer and Clayton. I wonder who that would be, Maven? Where were you earlier today?"

Maven smiled, unaffected by the sheriff's confrontation. "I was at Maven's Haven all day with Maddie. A bunch of folks saw me there. You're barking up the wrong tree, Dan." She looked over his shoulder. "Speaking of barking, I think your girlfriend's here."

"And her little dog too," said Maddie, in her best Wicked Witch of the East voice.

Sure enough, Jennifer pushed her way through the group, still holding Princess in her arms. She came to stand at the sheriff's side and whispered for all to hear, "I'm not gonna be left out. *Everyone's* here, Dan."

Violet would treasure the memory of the look

on Sheriff Winter's face for a long time. He took Jennifer's elbow and hustled her off to a corner for what looked to be a heated conversation.

Violet spied Kai Wauneka getting ready to leave and tugged Hugh's sleeve. "We have to catch the vet!"

They rushed over to Kai and Hugh set the cage on top of a side table. He uncovered it to reveal the plucked and cowering Edward. The vet nodded and then held up a finger for them to wait. They watched him go speak to the nurse at the reception desk who went away and came back with an apple. He pulled out a pocket knife and cut off a few slices, then unlatched the cage and slowly reached in to offer the bird some fruit. Edward eyed him suspiciously but reached out and took a slice with his beak and began to nibble it.

"I'll need to take him or her back to the clinic for a checkup and some hydration," said the vet, replacing the blanket.

Hugh raised an eyebrow. "I didn't even think about the fact that I might have an–Edwina."

"We'll see," said Kai. "Hey Violet, you're not going back out to the mesa tonight, are you?"

Hugh put an arm around Violet's shoulder. "I've been thinking the same thing. I don't think it's safe, with a killer running loose. Why don't we fire up that old Winnebago of yours and you can come stay at Maven's for a while?"

Violet melted into Hugh. "I can't think of anything I'd rather do. I don't want to be alone out there. But I need to check on Rosa first."

Kai nodded his head down the hallway. "She's

in with Clayton."

Violet walked down the hall to the one big hospital room where she had spent some time a few months ago. She peeked through the window into the darkened room and saw Rosa standing next to Red Clayton's bed, fluffing up his pillows and fussing over him. Red smiled up at her like a contented little boy. He had his Rosa back.

Rosa noticed Violet and put her hand over her heart, the way Violet had when Hugh drove off angry. Violet knew what she meant. Love.

Turning to go, she almost ran headlong into the beautiful doctor and mayoral candidate, Tamara Goodwill. Violet hardly recognized her with her bohemian clothes traded in for scrubs and her hair covered in a plain blue bandana. The doctor gave her a quick smile and headed through the door to check on her patient.

"Hey, Goodwill," Red croaked from his hospital bed. "Coming to finish off your competition?"

"I could have done that in the operating room, Clayton. When I win the mayor's race, it'll be fair and square. Now settle down, you need your rest."

Hugh came to stand next to Violet and took her hand. "We have a lot to do to get you moved to Maven's. We'd better go."

She kept hold of his hand and they walked out to the parking lot. A news van was just pulling in and the reporter, Cody Blackstone, jumped out, closely followed by his cameraman.

At that moment, Sheriff Winters exited the

hospital. The newsman pounced on him immediately.

"Hey sheriff! Is it true there's another serial killer on the loose?"

Sheriff Winters kept walking toward his cruiser. "What do you mean another?" he grumbled.

Blackstone and the cameraman followed the sheriff right up to the door of his car. "Someone killed Mr. Dewer and shot Red Clayton. And then there's the White Feather Killer. Isn't that two serial killers, sheriff?"

The anger, stress and domestic disputes of the evening showed on the sheriff's face. Violet almost felt sorry for him. "White Feather?" he said with irritation. "That's a different jurisdiction. You'll have to talk to the feds about that."

"Some folks are saying you botched the investigation, and now you're passing it off? Is that true, sheriff? Could Rainy Wauneka's death have been prevented? Are the women of Coatimundi and White Feather safe?"

Violet thought this might be the breaking point for Winters. But he took a deep breath, exhaled and climbed in his vehicle. "The White Feather Killer? That's a mystery, you got me on that one, Blackstone. But Dewer's murder? Well I got that one all wrapped up. And here's a little bit of breaking news for you. We're getting ready to make an arrest."

CHAPTER 21

Flames crackled in the fire pit in front of Hugh's RV. The group of friends huddled close, partly due to the chill and partly the general creepiness surrounding the day. The smoke of the fire mixed with the crisp smell of sage and desert night.

"'We're getting ready to make an arrest', those were his exact words?" asked Maven, her brows drawn and her face absent of its characteristic humor.

Hugh nodded. "I'm afraid so. But he didn't elaborate. Perhaps they have some new information."

Maven shook her head. "Nope. My goose is cooked. If we don't figure out who really killed that Dewer guy soon—"

Maddie took Maven's hand. "Don't even say it. We're gonna figure this out." The two women looked at Violet, who gulped. She felt the weight of responsibility on her shoulders and wished fervently that she could offer some insight.

"I was leaning toward Clayton," said Kai. The vet had driven the neglected parrot to his clinic in White Feather and returned with his sister Grace to help get Violet moved to Maven's Haven.

"But I doubt Red Clayton would shoot himself

in the arm," Kai continued. "He doesn't have the guts."

There were nods and murmurs from the group. Bella sat on the other side of the fire from Violet, her chair nuzzled close to Gabriel who had come to help with the move. Violet noticed a change in Bella that evening. She seemed positively sweet and even smiled when Violet thanked her for watching Spirit.

"Tomorrow's the opening night of Deep Dish," said Violet. "I won't have a moment to spare, between the cooking and decorating. But it will be a good chance for me to think over all the information we have. I feel like the answers are in front of me, but I just need to put them together."

"I'll be there to help, too," said Hugh. "And Bella's a whiz at decorating. She's an art major at NYU."

Amazingly, the girl nodded in assent.

Violet sighed. "I feel bad putting on a party tomorrow night when my dear friend is in trouble. Maybe I should postpone the opening."

Maven jumped up. "Not on your life, Violet Vaughn. You've worked too hard for this. Tomorrow's your moment. Don't you worry about me. I didn't kill Dewer and I didn't shoot Clayton. The wheels of justice turn slowly in Coatimundi, but it's all gonna work out in the end. I'll be there to help out tomorrow in whatever way I can. I know this little shindig is a costume party. Maddie and I already got our getup all worked out—and don't be askin', it's a surprise."

Everyone laughed and the tense mood was broken as everyone began to chat about the upcoming party.

Hugh held a carafe of hot chocolate that Violet made using her special Mexican cocoa. He proceeded to top off everyone's mugs. "The finishing touches for mine and Violet's costumes came in the mail today." He waggled his eyebrows. "But I guess you'll all have to wait and see."

Violet inhaled steam from the intoxicating brew in her mug and checked an incoming text from Rosa.

"Looks like Rosa's gonna stay out at Clayton's tonight with Bailey," Violet said to the group. "With Red in the hospital and Brody working, Rosa doesn't want her to be alone. They've got some ranch hands keeping a watch outside."

"Well, one's thing's certain," said Hugh as he put another log on the fire. "You might need to look for another cook."

Violet nodded. "I've already been thinking that. Rosa's heart is out at the Clayton Ranch."

"Clayton's always bragging around town about her cooking," said Maven. "Maybe he'll put his money where his mouth is and give her a big fat raise."

"I have an idea," Grace put in. "I'm teaching that traditional Navajo cooking class. I'd bet there's several people who'd be interested in the job."

Violet looked up to the sky in thanks. "That would be fabulous."

"Good," said Grace, smiling. "Anyone who's interested, I'll bring them with me tomorrow."

"There is one mystery that was solved today," said Kai, who stood and put a hand on Hugh's shoulder. "Edward is an Edward, not an Edwina. Hugh is the proud papa to a baby boy. Or a kid anyway. I put his age at about eight or nine years old. African Grays can easily live into their eighties, so you now have a pet for life."

"Maybe I need to get some cigars," said Hugh, to which everyone laughed.

Kai sat back down and Violet scooted her chair close to his. "So, how's it going with Special Agent Montoya?"

A little color came into his cheeks. "Well…um… she's doing a good job working on my sister's case. They still don't have any major leads, but I feel like someone's doing something, so that makes Grace and me feel better."

"That wasn't what I meant, and you know it. I meant have you asked her out yet."

Grace pulled her chair in close to Violet as well. "Yes, I want to hear the answer, too."

"We all do," said Maven. "Just ask her out, Kai."

A cheer went up.

"Ask her to the opening of Deep Dish," said Bella. "Costume parties are so romantic, you could coordinate your outfits."

Another cheer.

"I'm not good at this stuff," said Kai, covering his face.

Hugh patted Kai's shoulder. "She likes you. And I'm known for having deep insight into the female mind."

His statement was met with guffaws and a

round of balled-up napkins thrown at him from the women in the group, including Bella, who said, "Whatever, Dad."

The friends were jolted out of their seats by a chorus of coyote howls from quite nearby. Their mournful sounds seemed to pull everyone back to the darker matters at hand and a quiet settled over them, especially Maven, who stared down into her mug.

A short time later, Hugh and Violet settled into the bench seats of the dining table in Violet's little RV.

Violet poured tea into both their mugs. "This is my first attempt at real English tea. I hope it's...what should I say, up to snuff?"

Hugh took a sip. "It's jolly good. Just right."

Violet let out a big sigh and settled into her seat. "I really wish I had better answers for Maven. Right now, I feel like all this information is jumbled up in my head. I need to organize my thoughts."

Hugh held up a finger. "One sec."

He got up and rummaged in one of Violet's cupboards. "I saw this when I was helping you put things away earlier." He pulled out one of the blank canvases he had given her a few months ago during the Mundi Madness festival.

"You want me to paint a picture?" asked Violet. "We both know I have no skills in that department."

"We are going to paint a picture," he said, rummaging again and pulling out a package of markers. "Of a sort."

He placed the canvas in a napkin holder on the

counter and pulled out a marker. Then he wrote at the top of the canvas: Suspects.

"I see what you're onto. Like in the mystery shows."

"Spot on," said Hugh. "Fire away."

"Well, I think we should start with everyone we saw out at Emerald Eyes the day Dewer was killed. So first—Mateo."

Hugh wrote Mateo's name on the canvas. "Motive?"

Violet thought for a moment. "Dewer just fired him."

"And the motive for shooting Red Clayton?"

"Red also fired him from his ranch-hand work. And Red disapproved of his relationship with Bailey."

"Exactly," said Hugh, writing the information next to Mateo's name. "Next?"

"Bailey Clayton. I guess her motive for killing Dewer was that he just fired her boyfriend. But that's a little weak. Write that in green. And I don't think she would shoot her father."

"She did have a motive, though," said Hugh. "Same as Mateo. Her father was standing between her and her boyfriend. I'll write that in green, too—green for weak motive."

For the first time in days, Violet began to feel like they were making progress and her thoughts began to clear. She rested her chin in her hand and brought her thoughts back to the hot springs.

"Next, we saw Red Clayton talking to Dewer."

Hugh nodded and wrote Clayton on the board.

"His motive was stopping the development. He was in over his head and things were spiraling."

"And, his wife threatened to cut him off if he continued to engage in questionable business," Violet added.

"Agreed. And the motive for shooting himself?"

"I wouldn't put it past him to injure himself to deflect the blame," said Violet. "Maybe he felt the investigation was getting too close to him."

"Speaking of Clayton's wife...what about her?"

"I guess that's a possibility. We don't know anything about her, but she certainly has motive. Write her down with a question mark."

Violet looked the list over. "We also can't forget the man Bailey said she saw. An old guy with white hair. Although with kids, anyone over forty is probably an old guy to them."

Hugh wrote "old guy, white hair" on the board. For motive, he wrote a question mark.

"We also need to put Maven and Tamara here," he said, writing in their names. "Maven wanted to stop the development—that gave her a motive to kill Dewer and Clayton."

"Tamara had the added motive of getting rid of her mayoral competition—but write that in green. I don't think Tamara would risk her position for such a silly thing—or Maven either."

"That just leaves one person," said Hugh. "Our friend Prior Kenneth."

Violet set down her teacup. "No way. I just don't think a man of the cloth would—"

"You never know," said Hugh. "There's something else that points to him."

Violet raised an eyebrow. "That is?"

"He has white hair."

CHAPTER 22

After Hugh left, Violet sat down on the bench seat and continued to study the suspect list. So this is what she had to work with? More than half the people on the list were friends, or at least, people she liked. Spirit rested his head on the edge of the seat next to her and let out a sigh. Violet patted his head. "I know, buddy? It's troubling. And you know what I'm most troubled about?"

Spirit lifted his head and tilted it to one side, expectantly.

"Usually I have a feeling about things, you know? I don't have a feeling about any of these people. Except Maven. I know she didn't do it."

She shook her head a few times. "I'm sorry, bud, you probably just want to be fed."

She got up and opened a can of dog food and put it in Spirit's bowl.

"That's another thing. The restaurant. Deep Dish."

Spirit didn't even pretend to listen as he dug into his meal. Who could blame him? She probably sounded like a madwoman. But these felt like her first moments of clarity in weeks. Deep Dish is going in the wrong direction. There it was. The thing she'd been afraid to think.

Things were getting off track from her original, simple plan. How had that happened? The precious time leading up to her grand opening, she'd been distracted with the murder and getting Maven and Mateo off the hook. Things were spiraling and tomorrow was the day of reckoning.

Violet looked down at Spirit's empty bowl. "You wanna go to Deep Dish?"

He went ballistic at the unexpected chance to go somewhere. He jumped and barked, eyes bright and tail wagging.

Violet put on her coat, then paused a moment at the door. She should tell Hugh. But he'd want to come with her, or tell her not to go. The need to be alone with her thoughts won out. There were only twenty-four hours to get Deep Dish back on track. Another interruption from the murder, Red Clayton, Maven or any other dang Coatimundi problem might push her over the edge. Anyway, Spirit was there to protect her.

The office of Maven's Haven was dark, save for a small crystal lamp Maven always left on. There wasn't a person or car in sight this late at night. Violet began to wish she hadn't come. She crossed the highway, ran up to the door of Deep Dish, and got inside as quickly as possible. Locking the door behind her, Violet breathed a sigh of relief.

She flicked on the lights, went into the kitchen and looked around at the mouth-watering ingredients in baskets, bins and stacks. Shiny peppers, gnarled squash and juicy tomatoes. Chubs of salami and pepperoni. Rounds of aged cheeses. Jars of fresh-ground spices. The fridge was full of sausages sourced from local farms, free-range meats and crisp, fresh vegetables.

That was the problem. So many different flavors. She had tried to put them all into Deep Dish. But her original idea was to serve Deep Dish pizzas, not a Southwestern free-for-all.

"I know what I have to do," she said, mostly to herself, since Spirit was in the other room.

She began to pull out ingredients and gather them in groups on the center island–her most favorite flavors of the Southwest. She smelled and tasted each one. The pizza dough Rosa made that morning filled her senses with its tangy, sour smell as she pressed it into the mini pizza tins.

Violet, caught up in her work, barely noticed Spirit growling in the front room. How long had he been growling? The growl turned into a growl bark.

Violet froze. That was Spirit's warning bark. He had different barks for seeing another dog or spotting a rabbit. But this was the danger bark. She had only heard it once before–back when another murderer was running around town.

Wiping her hands on her apron, she picked up the largest butcher knife and peeked into the dining room. Spirit stood directly in front of the glass entry door. His ears lay back and his growl became louder. Violet crept closer to the door and tried to see outside, but it was difficult with the inside lights on. She wasn't about to turn them off. Flat against the wall, Violet crept closer to the door, holding the knife aloft. A shadowy figure approached the door. Violet saw a flash of white in the person's hands.

The assault on her restaurant gave Violet a rush of adrenaline. She jumped toward the door, knife in the air, and made the loudest, scariest sound she could think of, which ended up something between a roar and a pirate. "RAAAWRGGG!"

Her exclamation was met with an equally loud scream of fright, then rapid crunching of gravel as the villain ran away. Violet caught her own reflection in the glass and sucked in her breath. Her white apron looked like a crime scene, completely covered in spatters and smears of red pizza sauce. With the butcher knife in her hand, two words came to mind–psycho killer.

She pulled open the door and yelled, "Not at my restaurant!" Spirit pushed past her and ran outside. Violet followed close on his heels.

A piece of paper lay gleaming in the moonlight, dropped by the intruder. She half-expected it to be a flier for window cleaning or solar panels—in which case there'd be some apologizing to do. But something told her it wasn't. There was something familiar about that shadowy figure.

She snatched the paper from the ground. MIND YOUR OWN BUSINESS it said in black marker. It was very similar to the note Prior Kenneth received. If Hugh were here, he would point out that it must be the same writer, due to the lack of creativity.

The piece of paper fluttered. Her hands were shaking. Spirit had run to the edge of the road. His head moved back and forth between Violet and something out in the distance.

"Come on," she said. "Don't worry, he's not coming back. I scared the bejeezus out of him."

Spirit took one last look up the road and then trotted back to Violet's side.

Back in the restaurant, door locked, she eased herself into a dining chair. The cry of fright definitely sounded masculine. It had to be the killer. That ruled out a few people on the suspect list.

Violet fumbled in her apron for her phone and dialed Hugh. Within minutes, he was at the door of the restaurant, a jacket over his pajama pants and T-shirt, his hair a bed-head mess. Even though she was shaken up, Violet noticed he looked, frankly— adorable. Although, now that he was inside, his face showed some signs of suppressed anger, his mouth set in a hard line.

Violet headed him off at the pass. "I know. Seriously, I know. You're gonna say what was I thinking? There's a killer on the loose and I'm traipsing around town at midnight, not telling anyone where I'm going—"

And then, Hugh's arms were around her, pulling her close. She buried her face in his shirt and melted into the spicy-smelling, soft warmth that was—what did Rosa say? It was the simple thing she had known all along. Love.

"Violet Vaughn," he said softly, his mouth next

to her ear. "You are—"

Violet decided she'd better kiss him now, before he said anything else. And she did. A long, lovely, passionate, perfect first kiss.

"What am I?" she said, finally.

He squeezed her tighter. "Absolutely perfect."

CHAPTER 23

Later, they sat across from each other at one of the restaurant tables, eating fresh-baked chocolate cake. She gave Hugh a play-by-play of her encounter with the prowler and showed him the threatening letter.

"Definitely the same writer," he said, shaking his head. "So very trite. We need to call this guy the hackneyed assassin."

"Or...the clichéd killer?"

"That's it! We can suggest that for the title of Prior Kenneth's book."

"Unless he's the clichéd killer himself."

"You know you need to report this to–"

Violet was already shaking her head before he finished his statement. She held up a finger. "Don't say it."

"Sheriff–"

"Nope. That man will probably twist it around. He'll say Maven was just across the street, so it was probably her."

"I'll phone Montoya in the morning," Hugh said. "It could be an important piece to the puzzle. Now, let's get back home."

They stood together in the doorway as Violet locked up. The sound of a car screaming up the highway pierced the night. Violet called Spirit over and held his collar. The pickup that sped past was practically a blur.

"Geez," said Violet. "Some people."

Hugh ran out to the road.

Violet came to stand next to him. "What is it?"

"A white pickup. Coming from the direction of White Feather, exceedingly fast." He rubbed his hands through his hair. "Makes me wonder. It's been awhile since the White Feather Killer struck."

Violet took his hand. "There are a lot of white trucks around here. Come on, let's go home."

He put an arm around her waist and squeezed. But even in the dark, she could tell Hugh was troubled. Knowing how good his instincts were, it troubled her, too.

She placed a hand on his arm. "It seems we're destined to be constantly interrupted by villains."

"That's spot on. But at least I got my kiss this time."

CHAPTER 24

The morning of the grand opening began abruptly with a knock at the door. Violet, jarred awake, let out a groan. She was going to pay the price for the late night at Deep Dish. Right in the middle of a delicious dream, too. She and Hugh were walking hand in hand at the monastery and somehow they were also eating Navajo tacos. The bed in her little travel RV was a cozy nook where she'd always felt safe and secure. After her late night, she didn't feel ready to face the world yet. The knocking came again. Spirit stood in front of the door, tail wagging. A voice called her name. Hugh.

She stumbled out of bed and quickly checked her appearance. Blue silk pajamas, that was a plus, as it easily could have been sweatpants and an old Cubs T-shirt. She opened the door and knew right away something was wrong.

"What is it? Here, come in, I'll start some coffee."

Hugh climbed up the short step inside. "I can't stay. Something's happened. They think the White Feather Killer struck again last night. I knew it. I had a feeling when I saw that truck."

Violet put her hand to her chest in shock. "What happened? Was it another young woman from White Feather?"

"Yes, but she survived. She jumped out of his truck and another car happened to come along so the scoundrel took off. She's in the hospital in critical condition."

Violet sat down at the table. "Oh my gosh, that poor woman. Do you know who it is? Do we know the family?"

"I don't know much yet. Kai just called me a few minutes ago. But I'd really like to get on the scene. This might be a chance to learn some new details so we can finally catch this guy. I'll find out more when I'm there. Kai told me something else, too. Montoya told him Sheriff Winters still doesn't have enough to charge Maven. But he desperately wants to. And I guess they figured out Red Clayton's gunshot wound was not self-inflicted. Someone did shoot him."

Violet closed her eyes and tried to process all this new information. She blew out a breath. "That's— a lot."

"Indeed. I'm sorry to spring everything on you so early. I know it's your grand opening today. I'll be back later and Bella will be over pretty soon to help with the decorating."

"No, it's okay, you have to go. We'll manage here fine."

"Also, I'll probably see Montoya today. I think I should take her that evil note from last night."

Violet retrieved it from the kitchen counter.

She had placed it in a sealable plastic bag. "The writer wanted me to mind my own business. It's obviously someone who doesn't know me too well."

The corner of his mouth twitched up. "Do your best to stay away from trouble today while I'm gone. There's a lot of peculiar stuff going on right now."

Violet let out a nervous laugh. "I can assure you, I want nothing to do with any trouble."

"Just—keep your wits about you."

"Got it."

Hugh stepped closer. "One more thing. And this is really important."

Violet leaned in, expectantly.

"You look ravishing."

Hugh took Violet's hand and pulled her in for a kiss. When they drew apart, her head was reeling and she momentarily forgot why Hugh was even there. She shook her head to clear it, then squeezed his hand.

"Be safe. And let me know as soon as you find something out."

Violet got ready quickly and headed over to Deep Dish. The desert sun shone brilliantly on an unseasonably warm day. How could anything go wrong on a beautiful day like this? It was time to clear her mind and focus all her energy on the restaurant.

She halted at the curb to take in the view of her establishment. The plain white of the small building set off the glorious focal point—a large, retro-looking neon sign created by an artist friend of Maven's. "Deep Dish" appeared in the center in script writing, surrounded by green and yellow circles.

Violet folded her arms and felt her heart swell. So much had happened in the past few months. After finding out she'd been cheated by her estranged husband, her entire life had been turned upside down. But her life in Chicago had been lonely, boring and loveless. Now she had friends, adventure and–especially and–Hugh.

Now, the city girl stood in front of her very own restaurant in a tiny desert town with the strange name. She felt the circle closing as her ties to home shone in neon. Everything was absolutely perfect. Except...there was that note delivered to her last night. What was it about that note that tweaked something in her memory? And she still hadn't been able to do a thing to help get Maven off the suspect list.

Spirit nuzzled her hand, and she remembered how much still needed to be done. She patted his head. "I hear ya. There's only so much I can do in a day. Let's go."

Shortly after she unlocked the front door, Gabriel arrived, accompanied by Hugh's daughter, Bella. Their arms were laden with pumpkins.

"I just swung by Bella's place to give her a ride," he said, looking slightly embarrassed.

Violet raised an eyebrow. All the way across the street? Better not say it. Why fracture the small truce with Bella.

"Come see what I brought," said Gabriel, as he and Bella set down the pumpkins.

Violet followed them to Gabriel's car. The entire trunk and back seat were full of pumpkins.

"Wow, this is going to be amazing! Do I need to give you some money for these?"

"No, I got them for free. Uncle Kyle delivers peppers to the monks out at the monastery and they gave him some of the ones they didn't sell."

Soon Bella sat at a table covered in plastic so she could start carving.

Violet hovered over her shoulder. "Are you sure you don't mind doing this?"

"Are you kidding? This is heaven. I could carve pumpkins all day."

"You just might be doing that, judging by how many there are. But thank you. Oh, and save some of the seeds for me—we can use those."

Violet busied herself in the kitchen, chopping vegetables and making sauce. A short time later, Grace Wauneka poked her head through the swinging doors, then entered followed by a petite woman in her forties, her black hair cut in a short, spiky pixie.

"This is one of my students from the Navajo cooking class," said Grace.

The woman stepped forward and offered her hand. "Sam."

Violet clasped Sam's hand and noticed a fresh tattoo on the woman's well-toned upper arm—a swallow in flight. "That's beautiful. I love birds."

Sam placed her hand over her arm. "It symbolizes returning home. I just recently moved back to White Feather to care for my mom."

"Wait 'til you hear where she was living," Grace put in.

Sam pointed at a tattoo on her other arm, the digits "312".

Violet's eyes went wide. "What? But that's—"

"Chicago, yeah. Where you're from. When Grace told me you needed help here, it seemed like destiny."

"Because you already know how to cook deep dish pizza?"

"No, because I need a job. But I'm a fast learner and I love pizza, if that helps."

The way Sam said "job" in the Chicago dialect gave Violet a little pang in the heart. That full circle she thought about earlier really was coming closed. "I think that's all that's required. We'll talk details later. Can you start now?"

Violet lost no time setting Sam to chopping and prep work. Then she pulled Grace aside.

"So what's happening in White Feather? Hugh said another woman was attacked."

"They're pretty sure it was the same guy, the one that got Rainey. But the woman hit her head pretty bad and hasn't regained consciousness. A witness saw a white truck speeding away. But there's not really any new information. Hugh says you two might have seen the same truck tearing through here last night, so that might be something. I swear, they're never gonna get this guy."

Violet pulled Grace into a hug. "They'll get him eventually. You'll get justice for your sister."

They pulled apart and Grace wiped her eyes. "What about the murder of Mr. Dewer? Any progress?"

Violet quickly filled Grace in on the mysterious visit from the clichéd killer.

"If the prowler was a man, it proves it's not Maven," said Grace.

"I wish it were that easy. The sheriff will never believe me. That's assuming I tell the sheriff, which I don't plan to."

"I don't blame you. You know I don't have a high opinion of him either."

Violet nodded, knowing that Grace thought the sheriff had not done enough about her sister's murder.

"Hugh's taking the note to Montoya. We'll see what happens."

Grace reached out and squeezed Violet's hand. "No more about this on your big day. Put me to work."

Violet gave Grace some cooking duties, then left the kitchen to check on the others. Bella had already produced several intricately-carved pumpkins.

Violet sat down at the table and watched the young woman work. "You're very talented. These are works of art."

Bella continued carving. "It's a way to apologize, I guess. I was a proper witch when I first met you."

"Not a witch. You're just protective of your dad. That's understandable."

"I thought…well, I thought he and Mum would get back together. But Mum called me yesterday. She's getting married. To Andre."

"Is that the guy who was your dad's best friend?"

"Oh, no. That was over ages ago. This is some guy she met on holiday in France."

Violet's eyes widened. "That must be a shock."

"Whatever. I just decided my parents are moving on—and I need to as well." The corner of her mouth quirked up. "Besides, I can see how happy Dad is."

Violet returned the smile. "I know you're going back to school soon, but I'm glad we've had some time together. And I know someone else who's hoping you'll come back soon."

Bella followed Violet's gaze to where Gabriel was setting up the point of sale system at the counter.

"He's cute," said Bella, turning back to the pumpkin and resuming her carving. "Very motivated. I like that."

Violet couldn't help but agree. Gabriel seemed on top of everything for their big night.

The front door opened and Rosa rushed through the door, followed by Mateo and Bailey.

"I'm so sorry I'm late. We took Mr. Clayton home from the hospital this morning. I brought these two to help out."

Those two did not looked thrilled.

"Wanna carve some pumpkins?" Bella called out. The teenagers looked relieved and joined Bella at the carving table.

Violet called Gabriel over. "Let's get to the kitchen. Now that Rosa's here, I have a major announcement to make."

Violet addressed her small kitchen staff. "After a lot of soul-searching, I'm changing our menu. I know it's last minute—but we can handle it. The food being prepped today is for all-new recipes."

Rosa and Gabriel showed looks of surprise.

"So...no tamales, no Southwestern quiche, no squash soup?" said Rosa.

"Exactly," said Violet. "I'm bringing Deep Dish back to its roots. Deep dish pizza. Some very special Southwestern pizzas, each one reminiscent of a special dish I've tried during my time here."

Violet handed out copies of the new recipes and retrieved the samples she made the previous night.

Sam took a bite of the Navajo taco pizza and nodded her head. "Yeah, baby...this is yummy.""

"Try this, Rosa," said Violet. "This one's inspired by your tamales."

Rosa nodded appreciatively, her eyes closing in rapture.

"And this one's for you, Gabriel. The sauce uses your uncle's special chili powder."

Everyone seemed thrilled with the new recipes. Violet felt a wave of relief.

Gabriel nodded approvingly. "People around here are gonna love it. But...are we still serving the chocolate cake? That's a crowd-pleaser."

"Yes, we're keeping the cake for dessert. Hugh

would never forgive me if I took that off the menu."

Rosa clapped her hands together. "Yes. Now we're talking. This is Violet Vaughn meets Coatimundi."

By the time afternoon rolled around, Violet thought she'd better go home to change into her costume. Outside, Gabriel, Bella, Mateo and Bailey, now seemingly the best of friends, worked together stringing up lights and setting up pumpkins.

Gabriel ran toward Violet. "Don't look! We want to surprise you."

Violet held a hand up to the side of her face and kept walking.

"I didn't see a thing."

The day was going perfectly. Everything seemed to be in place to make sure opening night went off without a hitch. Violet crossed the road toward Maven's Haven and her little RV, Spirit at her side.

"You know what, Buddy? This is gonna be a night we'll never forget."

Spirit stopped in his tracks to glance at her, and seemed to have a long-suffering look of patient dog on his face.

"What?" she said, looking back at him. "You don't think that's a jinx, do you?"

CHAPTER 25

Violet let out a gasp at the sight of Hugh in his costume. He clutched his hand to his heart at the sight of hers. They stood outside his RV, preparing to head over to Deep Dish.

"It looks even better than I was expecting," said Violet. "The perfect Robin Hood. It's so…you!"

He swept his feathered green cap off his head and gave a courtly bow. "And m'lady is the fairest Maid Marian in the land."

She laughed. "You're not gonna talk like that all night, are you?"

"Nay. Nary a moment longer."

"That's good, because I don't want to have to use this." She pointed to the rustic dagger at her waist, secured behind an ornate, medieval-looking belt.

He chuckled. "I guess it's never too soon for dark humor in Coatimundi. This place is the bloody definition of it."

"You got that right. But they'll be no mundi madness tonight." She adjusted her thin leather head band, her face determined. "Or so I proclaim."

Hugh acquired their costumes online from a Robin Hood reenactment group.

"You're no Disney Robin Hood," she said,

putting her hands on her hips and stepping back to take a closer look at the costume. "It looks more realistic. Scruffier."

"Yours too, he said, reaching out to touch her long, green wool dress. "More of an Action Marian than the frilly one."

"That's good, because this Marian's ready for some action. I mean, in the kitchen...not..."

Hugh raised an eyebrow.

Violet turned so he wouldn't see her blush. "Come on, we've got to get to the restaurant. Wait— are those real arrows?"

He turned around so she could see the small quiver on his back, the colorful feathered ends sticking out. A simple bow rested next to it, slung over his shoulder.

"Nice touch," she said. "You look right out of Sherwood Forest."

He tipped his cap. "I am from Nottingham, after all."

Hugh offered his arm and together they set off on the short walk. Once again a pang of growing love and contentment flickered inside her. Despite anything else going on in the world—she had this.

"I want to fill you in on what happened in White Feather later, when we have more time." Hugh said as they strolled the path.

"Grace already told me some of it, but yes, I want to hear all about it."

Hugh looked back toward her RV. "What about Spirit?"

"I'm leaving him home tonight. There's just too much going on. But I got him a big fat bone to keep him occupied."

However, she pointedly didn't look over at her RV, worried that Spirit would be peering out the window forlornly.

"What about Bella, is she coming soon?"

"She's already over there, with her costume on. She said they were working on a surprise for you. I think she's making some friends here. That makes me so happy. She might visit her old dad more often now."

His voice seemed a little thick and Violet squeezed his arm.

They crossed the parking lot in front of Maven's Haven then Violet stopped and lifted her nose into the air.

"Can you smell that?" A toasty smell carried on the breeze, the unique, unmistakable aroma of warm pumpkin.

Hugh inhaled. "It smells like...Halloween."

"Yes, it smells heavenly."

They set off again and soon Violet could see a warm glow from the direction of the restaurant. Deep Dish was alight in orange warmth. Lit pumpkins lined the path on both sides all the way up to the front door. The outdoor arbor sparkled, lit up with strings of white lights wound around the posts. Flames flickered in the outdoor fire pit. Along the curb sat eight pumpkins, each with a letter that spelled out the restaurant's name.

"It's...glorious," she said, pausing to take it all

in. Then she saw all the kids coming toward her, Gabriel, Bella, Mateo and Bailey.

"Surprise!" they called.

Gabriel, dressed as a pirate, ran up to Violet. "Do you like it? Bella designed the whole thing."

Bella, looking adorable in her Tinkerbell costume, smiled shyly.

"I told you she was talented," said Hugh, beaming.

Mateo stepped forward. "And I wanted to do something to thank you for helping my mom...and me." He and Bailey were still in their regular clothes. "Mom's in the kitchen. She said she doesn't want you to do too much cooking on your opening night."

"We're gonna go get changed into our costumes now," said Bailey. "And...get my dad. He really wants to come tonight. Is...that alright? You don't mind, do you?"

Violet gave her a reassuring smile and nod. "Everyone from Coatimundi is welcome here." Whatever feelings she had about Red Clayton, she couldn't exactly turn him away. He was a prominent member of the community.

"Thank you—all of you—for your help. The decorations are amazing."

The young people dispersed and Gabriel and Violet conferred about the plan for the evening. Gabriel had hired some local teens as servers and they were due to arrive shortly. On a normal day, people would be ordering their pizzas at the counter, but for tonight's party they would offer table service. Violet expected many of the guests would want to gather outdoors, so she put Hugh in charge of tending the fire and greeting the arrivals.

Violet found Rosa in the kitchen humming a cheerful tune as she stirred a pot of dark red sauce, a tall black witch's hat perched on her head. Sam worked at the center island, pressing dough into pans.

At the site of Violet in her costume, Rosa dropped the spoon, her hands flying to her cheeks. "I love it! You're a medieval lady?"

Violet gave a little curtsy. "Maid Marian."

"Oh yes, Robin Hood's girlfriend. I love it." Rosa leaned over to smell the sauce. "I also love this new sauce recipe."

Violet tied on an apron and tasted the savory confection. "Perfect."

Rosa looked over at the diligently-working Sam. "I'm so glad you're bringing someone else in. I... well..."

"You're going back to work for Clayton. I know."

"You do?"

"It was clear to me the day he got shot. You love that family, despite their faults."

Relief flashed on Rosa's face. "Yes, that's it. You understand. But I'm so grateful to you. A job, a place to live..."

"You helped *me* out. You've been working your tail off to get Deep Dish open. And maybe I can call on you if I ever need back up."

Rosa threw her arms around Violet and they hugged tight. "Absolutely."

A short time later, Gabriel poked his head through the door. "Some guests are already arriving. And we have our first order—a classic pepperoni."

A cheer went up from the women in the kitchen and they moved to start preparing the first pizza.

The next hours passed in a blur for Violet as more and more orders came in. She didn't even get a chance to look through the door into the dining room, but she could hear the growing din of voices, laughter and clinking glasses.

Finally, Rosa put a hand on Violet's shoulder. "I've got this. You need to circulate with the patrons."

Violet nodded and removed her apron. She emerged from the kitchens to a cheer from the indoor guests. People stood clustered in groups or sat with tables pushed together, drinking, laughing and eating. As planned, Gabriel had lowered the interior lighting to match the Halloween mood, candles glowing on each table. The room was a sea of costumes. Violet worked her way through the crowd, shaking hands and accepting compliments on the meal. Guest after guest held cheesy slices of pizza in their hands. Many of them closed their eyes blissfully or offered thumbs up as she passed. She spied two green foam cacti making their way toward her—Maven and Maddie. Their faces showed through round cut-out holes in the foam. Each cactus had a sign attached to the front, which read, "Save the cactus!"

Violet shook her head. "You don't give up, Maven."

"Give up?" Maven swayed a little and Maddie

held her arm to steady her. "Give up on our desert? I'd rather fall into the Djinn. Oops, did I say that? Well that's downright wrong of me." She hiccupped. "You know I didn't do the pushin' of that Dewer guy. Mighta thought about it. Might be secretly—or not so secretly —impressed by someone else's gumption—"

Maddie held a green foam arm in front of Maven's face. "Do you just want to go to jail? You're talkin' yourself there. Again. That sheriff's out for your blood."

"Who, Dan? He's not gonna arrest me, he's—"

Maddie leaned in and whispered in Violet's ear as Maven rambled on. "A little too much cactus juice. I'm trying to get her home."

Violet nodded. "Good luck. Have you seen Hugh?"

"He's out by the fire pit."

Violet continued making her way out the front door. Red Clayton sat at a table outside, holding court with some of the other ranchers. Red, arm in a sling, was dressed as a bandit with a bandana and black cowboy hat. Upon seeing Violet, he raised his hat in an exaggerated way and gave her a saucy wink.

Violet shook her head and chuckled. She couldn't really blame Rosa. For all his nefarious ways, there was no doubt Red Clayton had charisma.

Hugh stood next to the fire talking with two people Violet didn't recognize at first. The man wore jeans, a denim shirt, a big curly wig and held a paint palette. She looked close. It was Kai Wauneka dressed as the famous TV painter, Bob Ross. A beautiful woman stood next to him. She wore a traditional Mexican dress, her upswept hair full of bright flowers and her mouth painted vivid red. As Violet got closer, she recognized the voice. Special Agent Montoya. Kai had managed to get a date with her after all.

The agent's party banter did not match the floral exterior. "So yeah, we don't know if it's an auto or semi-auto, or maybe something modified. But the perp is a novice with guns. With that caliber and weapon, Clayton should be dead."

Hugh pursed his lips, looking thoughtful. "Perhaps the shooter only meant to scare Clayton, not kill him."

Violet reached Hugh's side. "Sounds like I'm missing out on quite the conversation." She inclined her head toward Montoya. "You look beautiful, by the way. Frida Kahlo, right?"

Montoya had drawn in thick eyebrows to match the features of the famous Mexican painter. She crossed her arms. "Yeah, well don't get used to it, it's a one-off. My division chief said if I don't take a night off, he's gonna come to New Mexico himself and make me. I don't want him out here breathing down my neck."

"You don't have to feel bad about taking a night off," said Kai, taking the risk of touching the prickly agent on the arm. "You work hard. If you work too hard for too long, you make mistakes."

Montoya gifted Kai a slight smile. "I know, I'm— working on it."

Maven and Maddie ambled up to the group, Maven bubbling over with cheer as Maddie tugged at her sleeve. "That's it, Mave, almost home, let's keep it moving."

"I wanna warm up by the fire," said Maven. "Oh look, here's Tamara and...some guy." She hiccupped again.

Sure enough, another pair of costumed guests approached the group at the fire—Dr. Tamara Goodwill and her date. Violet did a double take. Wait, was that...Fritz, the awkward astronomer from Coati peak observatory? When Violet visited the site, he said he had been out on a date. But with Tamara? It actually kind of made sense in a way. Tamara was a brilliant doctor and he was a scientist. It was probably a love affair of the mind. At any rate, she hoped he had forgiven her for using his telescope. She wondered if the handsome Kent was joining them as well.

They were dressed as mad scientists. They both wore lab coats and each carried a large glass beaker full of neon green glow sticks. Tamara's hair was teased into a voluminous afro with white streaks painted into it. Fritz wore a shaggy white wig that stuck out in all directions, ala Doc Brown from *Back to the Future*.

"Good evening, welcome," Violet said warmly. "Great costumes."

Tamara put on a confused expression. "Costumes? We came straight from work."

Violet laughed. "I'm sure administering to Red

Clayton's injuries is enough to drive anyone mad."

"Oh yes, he's milking the attention for all he can get. But he'll be able to say he got great care at Coatimundi Hospital. We had the pizza with hatch chilies and cheese, by the way. All I can say is—wow."

Violet clapped her hands together. "I'm so glad you enjoyed it—that's my personal favorite."

Violet turned her attention to Fritz "What's Kent up to tonight?"

Fritz's expression changed on a dime as annoyance crossed his face. And was that–fear? "How should I know? It's not my job to keep tabs on him," he grumbled.

Tamara's head swung around and she shot him a look.

"Oh," he said. "I'm supposed to be working on my–people skills. I'm not good at—this stuff."

"So we see," said Hugh tightly, putting his arm around Violet.

"We were just leaving," said Tamara. "Fritz says it's the perfect night to see Mars, so we're heading up to Coati Peak."

Tamara took Fritz by the arm and they turned to go, but Tamara caught Violet's eye and mouthed, "Sorry."

Violet gave a little shrug and a wave and watched them leave down the path.

"Gonna 'show her Mars', is that what they're callin' it now?" said Maven, a little too loudly. She swayed dangerously close to the fire.

"Come on, Mave," said Maddie. "Let's get you

home."

But before they could go, a car pulled up in front of the restaurant, right up into the gravel path. The group swung their heads in unison to see the sheriff's car, spotlight blazing.

Violet clenched her jaw. Oh no, no, no. Not tonight.

Sheriff Winters, accompanied by the flame-haired Deputy Brody Clayton, crunched down the gravel toward them, silhouetted in the spotlight. A silence fell, only broken by the indoor guests who were still oblivious to the disruption.

The sheriff shined his flashlight around the faces of the group by the fire, finally landing and staying on Maven. He smirked and shook his head.

"What's this all about, Sheriff?" said Montoya, pushing forward.

He gave Montoya a slow up and down gaze, taking in her costume.

She drew her shoulders back, put her hands on her hips and tilted up her chin. "I asked you a question, sir. What's your business here tonight?"

A small crowd began to gather as the indoor patrons filtered out to see what was going on. Violet looked around at the concerned looks on her costumed guests, the same faces that moments ago were colored with the enjoyment of good food and friends. Anger burned in her belly, along with the fearful realization of what Winters was here to do. She had been too late to help her friend.

The sheriff shined his flashlight back on Maven

in her cactus suit. "It would appear my business is locking up some wildlife. Maven Jones, I'm arresting you on suspicion of the murder of Gavin Dewer and the attempted murder of Red Clayton."

CHAPTER 26

After a beat of silence, pandemonium broke out. Maddie screamed and clung to Maven's arm. The crowd reacted with collective "boos" and calls of "you got it wrong, sheriff". Deputy Clayton and Sheriff Winters stepped toward Maven.

"Now, you look here, Dan Winters. Who are you to accuse me?" she slurred, pointing a green foam arm at the sheriff. "I've seen you drunker than a skunk, skinny dippin' out at Emerald Eyes, I've seen you—"

"I wasn't informed of this," Montoya interrupted, marching up to the sheriff. "This is a joint investigation. You have to clear it with my team."

"Go back to your party...*Special Agent*," the sheriff sneered. "Seeing as you're taking some, uh—" He looked at her costume again, "Time off. I went ahead and cleared it with your division chief."

Montoya gritted her teeth at the mention of her boss. "I'm not gonna pull rank and override you in front of your community," she said in a low voice. "But you'll see me soon."

The officers began to take Maven away. By now, Red Clayton and his posse had come to watch. He clutched his injured arm dramatically and called out, "I can't believe you did this to me, Maven. Maybe now we can level that eye-sore of a trailer park and put up some condos."

Maven stuck out a foam arm, and—it's a good thing the hand was covered.

Violet turned to Hugh. "I can't believe this." She broke away from the group and followed directly behind the sheriff, seething.

"This is some pointed timing," she called at the sheriff's back.

Deputy Clayton began to put Maven into the squad car. She waved a cactus arm in the air and crooned, "The party's ooo-ver."

"You did this on purpose." Violet continued. "To ruin my grand opening."

Winters turned to face her. "Nothin' of the sort, Deep Dish. You might find this hard to believe, but it's not all about you." He leaned in close and spoke in a low, menacing voice. "Ever since you came here, this town has turned upside down. I've got murders. I got the FBI breathin' down my neck. And I got deep dish pizza—Chicago-style pizza—flung in my face. I'm gonna lock up your friend, and if you're not careful, I'm gonna lock you up too. For impeding the course of justice."

The sheriff's car drove away, Maven's foam cactus face pressed against the window. Violet stood at the curb watching its taillights. Hugh came and put an arm around her shoulder. Patrons began to file past, heading for home, or someplace else. Maven was right—the party was over. Violet watched a determined Frida Kahlo striding toward her vehicle, talking on her cell phone, followed by Kai Wauneka. Poor Kai. His date was now over as Montoya was officially back in work mode.

"Hey Mrs. Vaughn," called a voice behind her. She turned to see Mateo and Bailey rushing toward her, joined by Gabriel and Bella.

"We've been trying to talk to you," said Mateo.

"I'm not sure if it's important," said Bailey. "But I saw the man from Emerald Eyes, you know, the one I saw on the day Mr. Dewer was killed. The one with the white hair. At least I think it was him. It was definitely the same hair."

Violet blinked a few times, trying to process the information. Hugh was quicker on the uptake. "Who is it? Where is he?" He scanned the area, but no one was left. The interior lights had been turned up. Rosa, Sam and the hired servers could be seen clearing tables inside.

"He left a few minutes ago," said Mateo. "With Dr. Goodwill."

Violet's skin prickled as she felt an electric charge course through her. Her mouth hung open as her gaze slowly took in her restaurant, brightly-lit with candles and lights. The wheels tuned in her mind as pieces fell into place. Of course.

"Thank you," she said to the kids. "That's the piece I needed." She grabbed Hugh's arm. "We have to go." She saw his mouth drop open to speak, but she stopped him. "I'll explain in a sec—get the car!"

She turned to Gabriel. "Thank you for everything, you did an amazing job tonight. Pay everyone out of tonight's take. And I need to ask one more favor." She dug in the pockets of her medieval dress. "Here's the key to my RV. Can you let Spirit out for a few minutes?"

"We'll take care of him," said Bella. "But where are you going? Is this some of your detective stuff?"

"I'm not a detect—" Violet let out a sigh. "Well, yes. Just following a hunch."

CHAPTER 27

Violet clutched the wheel and leaned forward to better see into the pitch black darkness on the winding road up to Coati peak. She had done her best to give a quick overview to Hugh as they drove, but he still seemed skeptical.

"I don't know if that Fritz character has it in him," he said. "He has atrocious manners, but murder?"

"I saw something up there that might explain things. But for now, all I know is Tamara's in danger."

"Maybe they're in on it together. It's pretty convenient for her. She was opposed to the development and her competition for mayor was almost eliminated in the process. I really think we should contact Montoya or Sher—"

"Don't say it. I don't want to hear that name again tonight. And tell them what? The whole thing sounds really crazy if you try to explain it to someone."

Hugh's diplomatic silence was louder than a pack of crooning coyotes.

Violet pulled into the observatory parking lot. The headlights hit on what appeared to be the lone car in the lot.

"So what's the plan?" said Hugh.

Violet tapped her fingers on the steering wheel and gazed up at the building. A few dim lights showed from inside, but everything else was in darkness.

"I just want to check on Tamara. And ask Fritz a few questions. If my suspicions prove correct, we'll contact Montoya."

As they approached the observatory, the moon moved out from behind some clouds and bathed the structure in light.

"This costume was perfect for the party, but now I'm feeling a might awkward for a confrontation," Hugh whispered as he struggled slinging the bow and quiver over his shoulder.

"You could have left those in the car," she whispered back.

"I need the complete outfit. Otherwise I'm just a man in tights."

Violet stopped and reached out for his hand. "Thanks for trusting me, yet again. Or, at least...going along with me."

He squeezed her hand. "I'm at m'lady's service. I only wish I had my Band of Merry Men."

"Kent didn't lock the door behind him when I was here. I can only hope Fritz does the same."

She reached out and tied the handle on the plain, unmarked door. It turned.

Hugh followed her inside and they stood for a moment in the long, dim hallway with the dorm rooms. It was completely silent, other than the mechanical hum of distant equipment.

"This way," she said.

At the staircase, Violet hitched up her long skirts and made her way slowly upward, on alert for any sound. She saw light coming from the window in the door at the top of the stairs. When she reached it, she put her hands on the push bar and it opened easily.

A light shown out of the office shared by Fritz and Kent. Giggling and low murmurs bubbled down the hallway toward Violet and Hugh. She pointed at the office door and then made her way closer.

When they reached the door, Violet peeked around the corner. Tamara sat perched on Fritz's desk. He leaned up next to her, the shaggy white wig discarded on the floor, his bald head gleaming under the florescent lights.

Tamara held one of Fritz's Star Trek action figures in her hand. "I can't believe you have the original Spock," she purred. "This is my dream figure."

"Geek love," Hugh whispered in Violet's ear.

"You're my dream figure," Fritz said, reaching out toward Tamara.

Violet burst into the room. "Get away from him, Tamara. You're in danger!"

The two jumped, clearly taken completely off guard.

Tamara held her hand to her chest, eyes wide. "Violet? What the…are you alright?"

"What's going on?" Fritz demanded, standing protectively in front of Tamara.

Violet pointed at Fritz. "That man killed Mr.

Dewer and shot Red Clayton. And I think he may have done something to his colleague Kent, too."

Both Fritz's and Tamara's jaws dropped. Fritz shook his head. "You're nuts, lady. You're completely off your rocker."

"Now wait just a minute," said Hugh, moving forward and pointing at Fritz. "There's no need for that."

Fritz smirked. "Whatever...Robin Hood. I'll play along with your little joke. That is what this is all about, right? A joke?"

"Yes, explain yourself, Violet," said Tamara. "Because I don't think it's funny."

Violet stepped forward. "I know it's hard to believe, but listen. I saw a letter on Fritz's desk. The observatory's going to be closed and his project ended. It's because of the light pollution the Emerald Eyes development would bring. The whole point of putting a telescope in the desert is to be away from city lights."

Fritz began to shake his head, but Violet continued. "See that note on his desk?" She pointed to the hard drive with the sticky note on it. "That's the same handwriting and the same marker as the threatening letters sent to Prior Kenneth and me. And —" Violet moved to stand next to the discarded wig and pointed at it dramatically, "There's this."

"A Halloween costume?" said Tamara, looking skeptical.

"No, it's a wig. Someone wearing this wig was spotted at Emerald Eyes Hot Springs around the time Dewer was murdered. When I visited here with Kent, I looked through the telescope and it was pointed right at the hot springs."

Tamara looked back and forth from Violet to Fritz.

The scientist rubbed his chin and let out a burst of laughter. "You got it wrong. First of all, I'm not worried about the project. I've been offered a teaching position at the university. I was already leaving because I'm sick of being stuck up here with—" he broke off, looking a little frightened.

Violet stared at him with one eyebrow raised and arms folded. "That's only a little piece of it. What about the rest?"

He pointed toward the desk. "This sticky note? I didn't write this." He lowered his voice. "Kent did."

Violet's thoughts began to race. Was it possible she had done the correct equation but had miscalculated slightly? And if she had, then the answer had to be...

"And the wig?" Fritz continued. "I needed a last-minute costume and I'd seen the wig in Kent's closet, so I grabbed it. The person obsessed with the project here is Kent, not me. He's practically...unhinged about it. He's–"

"Unhinged am I?

All heads swung to the doorway where Kent stood. Violet had forgotten just how big he was. He looked different than the last time she had seen him. His hair was unkempt and stubble showed on his face. But that wasn't the scariest part. He held some type of large, camouflage-painted gun. It was large enough that he needed both hands to hold it. And it was pointing at all of them.

CHAPTER 28

"Tell us how you really feel, Fritz," Kent said. "But then again, you always do, don't you? You never cared about our work here. And we're this close–" he held his thumb and forefinger together in front of his face, "To a major breakthrough. Imagine it–me, Dr. Kent Simmons, to be the first person on Earth to confirm life on another planet."

He waved the gun around in the air as he talked, causing them all to cringe away from him and back up toward the window.

"What are you doing with a gun like that?" Fritz stammered. "You're a scientist...not flipping... Rambo."

Kent moved further into the room. His eyes scanned the group, moving erratically from one face to the next. "I had to stop that development. For the good of all mankind." He pointed his gun at the telescope. I stood right there, looking at Emerald Eyes and wondering what to do, how to stop it. And what do you know, there was Mr. Dewer, poking around down there."

Violet grasped Hugh's hand. They were trapped in this room with Kent with no way out. She had to stall for time until one of them could devise a plan. Clearly, there wasn't anything Kent wouldn't do to protect his project. But Violet doubted he would murder them all here in this office—it would be too messy and would threaten himself and his precious research.

"So you drove down there to confront him?" said Violet. "I'm certain you didn't plan to harm him... right?"

"No, I wasn't planning on harming anyone. But when I found him standing next to the Djinn, it was just...too easy. He was right next to it, taking pictures. He didn't even see me coming. So...just a little push was all it took."

Violet shuddered. It was cold-blooded murder.

"Why the wig?" Hugh ventured, pointing at the mop of white hair on the floor.

"One of the college kids left it behind after a Halloween party last year. I was worried Fritz might look through the telescope and I didn't want him to recognize me. But now...it doesn't matter."

"You shot Red Clayton as well," said Violet. "Were you just trying to scare him off the project?"

Kent chuckled, which, under the circumstances, sounded pretty creepy. "No, I actually wanted to kill Clayton. He planned to move forward with the development, even after his partner was killed. Killing him would have been a favor to the community. He's a greedy little sucker. But I just got this little baby," he indicated the camo gun. "I got off one shot and then it jammed." He swung the gun back and forth between all of them. "But I won't make that mistake again. I've been practicing."

Tamara let out a little shriek and Fritz put his arm around her.

"Just let us go," said Violet, her voice sounding stronger than she felt. "You don't want to harm anyone else."

Kent let out a laugh. "Nice try. We both know it's a little late for that. My plans are finally coming together. I'll be famous. And no one is going to stop me. Let's go."

He kept the scary gun pointed at them and motioned toward the door with his head. This must be the automatic weapon Montoya was talking about. He didn't need to be accurate with a gun like that. In an instant, they could all be dead.

"Leave your cell phones and keys on the desk," he barked.

There wasn't much they could do to defy him in the small office. Their best hope was to get out of the building and maybe overpower him. Violet reluctantly pulled her phone out of her pocket and placed it on the desk. She met eyes with Hugh. He had that nonchalant British swagger that made it appear this was just another minor inconvenience. He gave her a quick wink. Did he have something up his sleeve, or was it just a wink of encouragement?

Tamara let out a sob as she set her phone and keys on the desk. The doctor was truly terrified. Fritz patted her shoulder and put his things down as well. Violet felt a wave of guilt at suspecting him.

Kent dumped the phones and keys into a backpack, then ushered them out of the facility. He walked behind them as they proceeded single file out into the cold Halloween night. The full moon, high in the sky, allowed them to occasionally see their environment when the clouds parted. Kent held a powerful flashlight that blinded them if they looked in his direction. It lit up a swath in front of them.

"Head around the building and down the path." Kent said. "Let's go."

They picked their way slowly down a trail that ran behind the observatory, skirting a rocky cliff face. Brush and thorny cactus spotted the narrow, pebbled walkway and tore at Violet's long skirts.

The path became even narrower. On one side they were pinned in by the flat cliff face. On the other was blackness that indicated a steep drop off.

Suddenly, the light illuminating the trail disappeared followed by a curse from Kent. He must have dropped the flashlight.

"Run!" Hugh's voice called from behind her. Ahead, she could hear Tamara and Fritz scrambling. Violet rushed forward as quickly as she could. She felt along the rocks with her hands, stumbling.

Then, from behind her, she heard crumbling rock and an "oof" from Hugh. She spun around. The moonlight gleamed on the empty path behind her. Hugh was gone.

CHAPTER 29

Oh no. No, no, no. "Hugh," she called out. Her heart pounded. She could see the bright flashlight in the distance heading toward her.

"It's all right, I'm down here." Hugh's whisper came from somewhere below her, off the side of the path. She swayed for a moment as relief overwhelmed her.

"There's another path down here," he whispered. "Quickly, follow my voice."

Violet got onto her hands and knees and felt along the edge of the rocks. Finally, she felt Hugh's hand and slid over the edge, landing on top of him, both of them falling to the ground. He put his arms around her and they watched the light from the flashlight momentarily glint on the rocks above and then disappear.

"We need to get back to the observatory," said Hugh. "There must be a phone or computer we can use."

A scream pierced the night.

"That's Tamara," Violet whispered. "We have to help them."

Hugh let out a shaky breath. "Okay. I'll go help.

You go back to the observatory."

"No way." She took both his hands. "We stay together."

Hugh nodded. "Alright then. This way."

They doubled back down the new path and soon found a place where they could climb back up to the higher trail, moving as quickly as they could in the semi-darkness. They didn't have far to go. The trail led around a curve in the mountain and opened into a clearing. At the far end of the area was a precipice that jutted out over a canyon. Fritz and Tamara were making their way closer to the edge, spurred on by the gun-wielding Kent.

Violet and Hugh followed behind. As they closed the distance, Hugh took Violet's hand and pulled her down behind a cluster of rocks. Fritz and Tamara had reached the edge of the cliff. Kent shined the light in their faces. They squinted and shielded their eyes.

"For the love of God, Kent, stop this!" yelled Fritz. "You don't want to kill us. Put the gun down."

"It's too late for that," Kent yelled.

"People know we came up here tonight," said Tamara. "You'll be a suspect if we're missing."

Kent shook his head. "All they'll know is that two couples came up here for a romantic stroll and—sadly—fell to their death when the precipice fell away. After I get rid of you two, I'll find that wanna-be detective and her limey boyfriend and they'll follow you over. They won't get far since the observatory is locked and they have no vehicles. Now, make it easy on yourselves and just jump. It's better that way."

"You'll have to push me over yourself, Kent," Fritz called.

Kent made to move toward them, but then a whoosh sounded in the air. Kent froze. He dropped to his knees, the gun and flashlight tumbling from his hands. He reached wildly to his back. There, in the moonlight, gleamed an arrow, sticking out of his shoulder.

Hugh was already up and running toward the injured Kent who was now flailing on the ground. Violet ran close behind, the antique dagger unsheathed and in her hand. Hugh's toe caught a rock and he went tumbling. Violet looked back and forth between Hugh and Kent. The scientist was reaching for the gun. Violet leapt toward him and kicked it out of his reach. But Kent grabbed her foot and let out an animal growl. He pulled Violet to the ground. She slashed at him with the dagger, but Kent was much stronger, even injured. He held her wrist and they ended up rolling around in the dirt, dangerously close to the edge of the cliff.

Fritz and Tamara ran to help, pulling on Kent's shoulders to get him off Violet. With one final pull, they wrenched him loose and he fell onto his back. Violet scrambled away, feeling cactus thorns tear into her skin. She tried to catch her breath, her heart beating out of her chest. She raised her head to see Hugh standing over Kent, arrow fully loaded and pointed at the man's chest.

"Now, old chap," he said, slightly out of breath,

but still with trademark charm. "Who are you calling a limey?"

Violet pushed herself off the ground and came to stand next to Hugh. "Don't tell me." She placed a hand on his shoulder. "Archery team at uni?"

Hugh kept the bow taut, looking for all the world like Robin Hood himself had fallen out of the pages of a book—although he had lost his feathered cap some time back. "Yes, m'lady. Team captain."

CHAPTER 30

Violet looked at the friends gathered around the table at Deep Dish and decided her life was complete. Hugh chatted with Kai and Montoya. Grace and Rosa were deep in conversation about a tamale recipe. Tamara, a bandage on her head, sat next to Fritz, who, Violet had to admit, was trying to work on his social skills. The two of them sported "Vote for a Better Tamara" gear from head to toe.

Maven regaled anyone who would listen about her stay in the Coatimundi jail. "Now don't anyone go sayin' anything, but that Deputy Jones is a keeper. He brought me a doughnut and we passed the time playin' poker through the bars." Maddie looked on with a huge smile, finally getting back to herself after Maven was cleared.

It was Election Day. Banners and balloons, both blue and red, festooned the restaurant. Although Violet had a personal favorite, she had decided to make the occasion non-partisan. Patrons from every side of the aisle filled the place. The TV blared all the New Mexico election results. Reporter Cody Blackstone filled the screen, interviewing candidates at a much larger venue. It took awhile for the crawl at the bottom of the screen to get to tiny Coatimundi. But when it did, a cheer rang out and Tamara stood up to receive pats on the back and hugs. Red Clayton got up from his chair and came to stand in front of her, his arm still in the sling.

"Sympathy votes," he said. But he had a twinkle in his eye. "Well, if it wasn't me, I'm glad it was you, doctor. They tell me you saved my arm. So, I guess losing to you was the least I could do. I give you... Mayor Goodwill!"

Tamara shook his hand, and the two became lost in a crowd of well-wishers.

Violet touched Hugh's arm. "I'm gonna go check on the animals."

"I'll come with you."

Violet patted Gabriel on the back as they passed him at the register. He looked over his shoulder. "Did Bella make it home okay?"

"Yes," said Hugh, "she got to New York in one piece."

Gabriel's love-lorn feelings showed on his face. Hugh clapped him on the back. "Don't worry young man, she's planning to come back for Christmas."

A smile lit Gabriel's face and all he could do was stammer, "Thank you...thank you."

Violet and Hugh pushed through the double doors to the kitchen. Sam had headsets on and was rockin' out while she tossed pepperoni on a pizza, one at a time. She gave them a nod and a wave.

Violet went to her little office in the back. She opened the door and Spirit bounded off of his dog bed. While Violet gave him some love, Hugh went to the large birdcage on the desk. Edward sat on a perch, eating a seed stick. He let out a high-pitched whistle followed by a series of what sounded like "glug glug glugs" to Violet.

"See that?" said Hugh. "He said hello. I heard it. Did you hear it?"

"Uh...sure," said Violet, "It could have been. What I do know is that he looks like a different bird. I love the little fluffy parts where his feathers are growing in."

"Yes, he's a good boy," said Hugh, putting his finger through the bar. Edward still wouldn't let anyone touch him, but he definitely seemed partial to Hugh.

Violet went to the back door of the restaurant and flung it wide. Spirit careened into the open desert, bounding over brush and rocks.

Hugh came to stand next to Violet at the door. "Montoya just told me that the last woman attacked in White Feather—she has no memory of the event. They're hitting dead ends everywhere."

Violet leaned into him. "What do you think?"

"I think he's escalating his behavior. That's what serial killers do."

"I know that Kai and Grace are so thankful for your help. We're gonna get him."

"We?"

"Yes. Now that I've solved my second murder case, I think I'm ready for the big leagues. We need to get that guy. This is my community now. This is where my friends are. This is where...you are. Let's get him."

They stood in silence and watched the sun setting over the desert, red, pink and purple.

"I meant to tell you," said Hugh. "I've had a call from Prior Kenneth, thanking us for our help in catching his brother's killer. He invited us both for a free stay at one of the monastery guest houses."

"Maybe they'll let us sit in on their mystery writers' group. I'd love to find out how their story's going to end."

Hugh gave her a squeeze. "You haven't had enough mysteries for awhile?"

Violet laughed. "In Coatimundi?"

She watched the last colors in the sunset fade and thought about the strange little town she was beginning to think of as home.

"Something tells me I'd better get used to it."

THE END